The
Elements of Style

英文寫作聖經

史上最長銷　美國學生人手一本
常春藤英語學習經典《風格的要素》

〔中英對照，附原版練習題＆實戰練習手冊〕

William Strunk Jr. 威廉·史壯克——著

陳湘陽——譯

目錄

—— CONTENTS ——

* 特別感謝譯者陳湘陽老師提供詳盡解答

前言

本書旨在介紹用簡明扼要的風格寫作英文文章的重點
規則。為了減輕教師和學生閱讀的負擔，我將著重於
講解幾個寫作的基本要素、文法規則，以及最常違反
的寫作原則。

同樣地，本書第二章中介紹的段落寫作手法，都是最
基本且廣泛運用的原則。也就是說，本書僅包含了整
體英文寫作風格的一小部分。根據我過去的經驗，學
生在習得寫作的基本知識後，再透過個別指導，從寫
作的錯誤中學習，將能有更顯著的進步，就這方面來
說，比起教科書提供的內容，教師可能更偏好從自身
的理論和經驗出發。

康乃爾大學英語系的同事們在我整理手稿時幫了許多
忙。George McLane Wood 先生很大方地允許我使用
他的文章〈給作者的建議〉中的素材，並將其加入本
書的規則 10。

INTRODUCTORY

This book aims to give in brief space the principal requirements of plain English style. It aims to lighten the task of instructor and student by concentrating attention on a few essentials, the rules of usage and principles of composition most commonly violated.

Similarly, it gives in Chapter II only those principles of the paragraph and the sentence which are of the widest application. The book thus covers only a small portion of the field of English style. The experience of its writer has been that once past the essentials, students profit most by individual instruction based on the problems of their own work, and that each instructor has his own body of theory, which he may prefer to that offered by any textbook.

The writer's colleagues in the Department of English in Cornell University have greatly helped him in the preparation of his manuscript. Mr. George McLane Wood has kindly consented to the inclusion under Rule 10 of some material from his "*Suggestions to Authors*".

以下書目為建議的延伸閱讀：

第一章及第三章可參考：

1. F. Howard Collins, *Author and Printer* (Henry Frowde);

2. Chicago University Press, *Manual of Style*;

3. T. L. De Vinne, *Correct Composition* (The Century Company);

4. Horace Hart, *Rules for Compositors and Printers* (Oxford University Press);

5. George McLane Wood, *Extracts from the Style-Book of the Government Printing Office* (United States Geological Survey)

第二章及第四章可參考：

1. Sir Arthur Quiller-Couch, *The Art of Writing* (Putnam), （特別是 Interlude in Jargon 這章）

2. George McLane Wood, *Suggestions to Authors* (United States Geological Survey)

3. John Lesslie Hall, *English Usage* (Scott, Foresman and Co.)

4. James P. Kelley, *Workmanship in Words* (Little, Brown and Co.).

The following books are recommended for reference or further study:

in connection with Chapters I and III,
1. F. Howard Collins, *Author and Printer* (Henry Frowde);
2. Chicago University Press, *Manual of Style*;
3. T. L. De Vinne, *Correct Composition* (The Century Company);
4. Horace Hart, *Rules for Compositors and Printers* (Oxford University Press);
5. George McLane Wood, *Extracts from the Style-Book of the Government Printing Office* (United States Geological Survey)

In connection with Chapters II and IV,
1. Sir Arthur Quiller-Couch, *The Art of Writing* (Putnam), especially the chapter, Interlude on Jargon
2. George McLane Wood, *Suggestions to Authors* (United States Geological Survey)
3. John Lesslie Hall, *English Usage* (Scott, Foresman and Co.)
4. James P. Kelley, *Workmanship in Words* (Little, Brown and Co.).

這些延伸閱讀詳述了本書中一些概略帶過的要點，並包含豐富的實例，能補充本書的不足之處。

根據我多年的觀察，傑出的作家有時會刻意違反既定的寫作形式。雖然他們犧牲了正確的格式，但那樣的書寫通常能讓讀者感受到其中的價值。除非寫作者有十足的把握，否則最好還是遵守寫作原則，我建議寫作者等到透過指導，有能力寫出日常生活的實用英文後，再去拜讀文學大家的作品，發掘各種寫作風格的祕密。

In these will be found full discussions of many points here briefly treated and an abundant store of illustrations to supplement those given in this book.

It is an old observation that the best writers sometimes disregard the rules of rhetoric. When they do so, however, the reader will usually find in the sentence some compensating merit, attained at the cost of the violation. Unless he is certain of doing as well, he will probably do best to follow the rules. After he has learned, by their guidance, to write plain English adequate for everyday uses, let him look, for the secrets of style, to the study of the masters of literature.

第一章

英文語法的 7 個基本規則

I

ELEMENTARY RULES OF USAGE

本章要教你用最簡潔的句式，
寫出清晰有力、邏輯通暢的好句子。
請務必精通規則 5「用分號形成複合句」，
這是最實用的寫作技巧之一。

第一章 英文語法的7個基本規則

規則 1
規則 2
規則 3
規則 4
規則 5
規則 6
規則 7

規則 1　單數名詞加「'」形成所有格。

不論名詞結尾的子音為何,請遵照這個原則,例如:

> Charles's friend　查爾斯的朋友
> Burns's poems　伯恩斯的詩
> the witch's malice　女巫的怨恨

這是美國政府印刷局和牛津大學出版社採用的規則,但也有些例外,包括結尾是 -es 或 -is 的古代專有名詞、Jesus(耶穌)的所有格 Jesus',以及 for conscience' sake(為問心無愧)、for righteousness' sake(為了正義)等用法。 不過,Achilles' heel、Moses' laws、Isis' temple 這類的用法經常由以下的書寫方式替代:

> the heel of Achilles　致命的弱點
> the laws of Moses　摩西的律法
> the temple of Isis　埃西絲神廟

Hers、its、theirs、yours、oneself 等代名詞所有格則不需要加撇號(')。

Form the possessive singular of nouns by adding 's.

Follow this rule whatever the final consonant. Thus write,

> Charles's friend
> Burns's poems
> the witch's malice

This is the usage of the United States Government Printing Office and of the Oxford University Press. Exceptions are the possessive of ancient proper names in *-es* and *–is* , the possessive *Jesus'*, and such forms as *for conscience' sake, for righteousness' sake*. But such forms as *Achilles' heel*, *Moses' laws*, *Isis' temple* are commonly replaced by

> the heel of Achilles
> the laws of Moses
> the temple of Isis

The pronominal possessives *hers*, *its*, *theirs*, *yours*, and *oneself* have no apostrophe.

I

ELEMENTARY RULES OF USAGE

RULE
1

RULE
2

RULE
3

RULE
4

RULE
5

RULE
6

RULE
7

規則 2 若有三個以上的詞語並列，其間只有一個連接詞，請在每個詞語後加上逗號，最後一個除外。

例如：

red, white, and blue 紅色、白色、藍色
gold, silver, or copper 金、銀、銅
He opened the letter, read it, and made a note of its contents. 他打開信件閱讀，並記下其中內容。

這也是美國政府印刷局和牛津大學出版社採用的規則。

運用在公司名稱上時，則省略最後一個逗號，例如：

Brown, Shipley and Company. 布朗與席普利公司

RULE 2 In a series of three or more terms with a single conjunction, use a comma after each term except the last.

Thus write,

red, white, and blue
gold, silver, or copper
He opened the letter, read it, and made a note of its contents.

This is also the usage of the Government Printing Office and of the Oxford University Press.

In the names of business firms the last comma is omitted, as,

Brown, Shipley and Company.

I

ELEMENTARY RULES OF
USAGE

RULE
1

RULE
2

RULE
3

RULE
4

RULE
5

RULE
6

RULE
7

規則 **3** 附加說明的內容，要置於兩個逗號之間。

The best way to see a country, unless you are pressed for time, is to travel on foot. 除非你趕時間，了解一個國家最好的方式莫過於徒步旅行。

這個原則較難應用，因為我們經常不易判斷一個字（例如 however）或一個簡短的片語是否屬於「附加說明」。若對句子的通順度影響不大，我們在寫作時可以放心地把逗號拿掉。但無論去除逗號對句子的影響是大是小，切記不要只去除一個逗號。以下兩句皆是錯誤的用法❶：

Marjorie's husband, Colonel Nelson paid us a visit yesterday.
瑪喬麗小姐的先生尼爾森上校昨天來拜訪我們。
My brother you will be pleased to hear, is now in perfect health.
你聽到應該會很開心：我哥哥現在身體非常健康。

學習小提醒 1

這兩句應該修正為：

Marjorie's husband, Colonel Nelson, paid us a visit yesterday.
My brother, you will be pleased to hear, is now in perfect health.

RULE 3 Enclose parenthetic expressions between commas.

> The best way to see a country, unless you are pressed for time, is to travel on foot.

This rule is difficult to apply; it is frequently hard to decide whether a single word, such as *however*, or a brief phrase, is or is not parenthetic. If the interruption to the flow of the sentence is but slight, the writer may safely omit the commas. But whether the interruption be slight or considerable, he must never insert one comma and omit the other. Such punctuation as

> Marjorie's husband, Colonel Nelson paid us a visit yesterday.
> or
> My brother you will be pleased to hear, is now in perfect health.

is indefensible.

I

ELEMENTARY RULES OF USAGE

RULE
1

RULE
2

RULE
3

RULE
4

RULE
5

RULE
6

RULE
7

如果附加說明的內容前面有連接詞，請把第一個逗號
置於連接詞前，而非連接詞後，例如❷：

He saw us coming, and unaware that we had
learned of his treachery, greeted us with a smile.
他看到我們走來，臉上掛著微笑迎接，渾然不知我們已聽
說了他背叛的行為。

以下項目不管出現在何處，皆視為附加說明，須置於
兩個逗號之間（或逗號與句號之間）：

(1) 年份與日期

February to July, 1916. 1916 年 2 月到 7 月
April 6, 1917. 1917 年 4 月 6 日
Monday, November 11, 1918.
1918 年 11 月 11 日星期一

(2) etc. 和 jr. 兩個縮寫❸

學習小提醒 2

這個例句常見的錯誤語法是 He saw us coming and, unaware that we had learned
of his treachery, greeted us with a smile.

學習小提醒 3

etc. 須置於兩個逗號之間的例句如：Karen tries not to eat chips, chocolate,
etc., even though she loves junk food.

If a parenthetic expression is preceded by a conjunction, place the first comma before the conjunction, not after it.

> He saw us coming, and unaware that we had learned of his treachery, greeted us with a smile.

Always to be regarded as parenthetic and to be enclosed between commas (or, at the end of the sentence, between comma and period) are the following:
(1) the year, when forming part of a date, and the day of the month, when following the day of the week:

> February to July, 1916.
> April 6, 1917.
> Monday, November 11, 1918.

(2) the abbreviations *etc*. and *jr*.

I

ELEMENTARY RULES OF USAGE

RULE 1
RULE 2
RULE 3
RULE 4
RULE 5
RULE 6
RULE 7

(3) 非限定關係子句，也就是功能非定義或區別先行詞的子句；由指涉時間（when）或地點（where）的連接詞帶出的類似子句亦然。

> The audience, which had at first been indifferent, became more and more interested.
> 一開始毫無興趣的聽眾，愈聽興致愈高昂。

在這個句子裡，which 開頭子句的功能並非告訴我們「是哪一群聽眾」，因讀者應已知道指涉的對象是誰；這個子句的功能是加入一段敘述，補充說明主要子句中的內容。

這個句子其實結合了兩個敘述，而這兩個敘述皆能獨立成句：

> The audience had at first been indifferent. It became more and more interested.
> 聽眾一開始沒什麼興趣；他們愈聽愈有興致。

對照未由逗號引導的限定關係子句：

> The candidate who best meets these requirements will obtain the place.
> 最符合這些條件的申請者將取得此職位。

(3) non-restrictive relative clauses, that is, those which do not serve to identify or define the antecedent noun, and similar clauses introduced by conjunctions indicating time or place.

> The audience, which had at first been indifferent, became more and more interested.

In this sentence the clause introduced by *which* does not serve to tell which of several possible audiences is meant; what audience is in question is supposed to be already known. The clause adds, parenthetically, a statement supplementing that in the main clause.

The sentence is virtually a combination of two statements which might have been made independently:

> The audience had at first been indifferent. It became more and more interested.

Compare the restrictive relative clause, not set off by commas, in the sentence,

> The candidate who best meets these requirements will obtain the place.

I

ELEMENTARY RULES OF USAGE

RULE
1

RULE
2

RULE
3

RULE
4

RULE
5

RULE
6

RULE
7

在此句中，who 開頭的子句功能在於指稱「是好幾個申請者中的哪一個」；這個句子無法分成兩個獨立的敘述。

以下兩個句子標點上的差別亦是根據相同的原則：

Nether Stowey, where Coleridge wrote *The Rime of the Ancient Mariner*, is a few miles from Bridgewater. 柯立芝創作〈古舟子詠〉的所在地下斯托伊村，離布里奇沃特只有幾哩之遙。
The day will come when you will admit your mistake. 你承認錯誤的那天終將到來。

Nether Stowey 是個專有名詞，無須多做解釋，因此關於柯立芝的那段敘述為補充／附加說明。相反地，第二個句子中的 day 則由其後的從屬子句修飾，為限定用法。

在一個句子中，由逗號引導的片語或從屬子句，不管是在主要子句之前或之後，採用的原則與「附加說明的內容，要置於兩個逗號間」類似，請見下頁例句：

Here the clause introduced by who does serve to tell which of several possible candidates is meant; the sentence cannot be split up into two independent statements.

The difference in punctuation in the two sentences following is based on the same principle:

> Nether Stowey, where Coleridge wrote *The Rime of the Ancient Mariner*, is a few miles from Bridgewater. The day will come when you will admit your mistake.

Nether Stowey is completely identified by its name; the statement about Coleridge is therefore supplementary and parenthetic. The *day* spoken of is identified only by the dependent clause, which is therefore restrictive.

Similar in principle to the enclosing of parenthetic expressions between commas is the setting off by commas of phrases or dependent clauses preceding or following the main clause of a sentence.

RULE
1
RULE
2
RULE
3
RULE
4
RULE
5
RULE
6
RULE
7

Partly by hard fighting, partly by diplomatic skill, they enlarged their dominions to the east, and rose to royal rank with the possession of Sicily, exchanged afterwards for Sardinia.

他們一方面驍勇善戰，一方面擁有良好的外交手腕，東方的領土因此日漸擴大。他們在擁有西西里後成為皇室的一份子，稍後更用西西里換得了薩丁尼亞。❹

其他例子請見規則 4、5、6、7、16、18 中引用的句子。

寫作者必須注意：獨立子句的前面不能有逗號，請見規則 5。

學習小提醒 4

此句中主要子句為 they enlarged...for Sardinia，補充說明的片語 partly by hard fighting 和 partly by diplomatic skill 則置於主要子句之前。

> Partly by hard fighting, partly by diplomatic skill, they enlarged their dominions to the east, and rose to royal rank with the possession of Sicily, exchanged afterwards for Sardinia.

Other illustrations may be found in sentences quoted under Rules 4, 5, 6, 7, 16, and 18. The writer should be careful not to set off independent clauses by commas: see under Rule 5.

RULE
1

RULE
2

RULE
3

RULE
4

RULE
5

RULE
6

RULE
7

規則 4　引導對等子句的連接詞前須加逗號。

The early records of the city have disappeared, and the story of its first years can no longer be reconstructed.
這座城市稍早的紀錄皆已消失，無法重建其早年的光景。
The situation is perilous, but there is still one chance of escape. 情況相當危急，但仍有一線生機。

以上兩個例句若脫離上下文可能得重寫，因為句子的意義到逗號前已經完整，使第二個子句看起來像「後來才加上去的」。此外，and 是個最不明確的連接詞；它只連接兩個獨立子句，卻未明示兩個子句間的關係。在上述例句中，前後子句間有因果關係，建議改寫為：

As the early records of the city have disappeared, the story of its first years can no longer be reconstructed. 因這座城市稍早的紀錄皆已消失，所以無法重建其早年的光景。
Although the situation is perilous, there is still one chance of escape.
即使情況危急，仍存在一線生機。

Place a comma before a conjunction introducing a co-ordinate clause.

The early records of the city have disappeared, and the story of its first years can no longer be reconstructed.

The situation is perilous, but there is still one chance of escape.

Sentences of this type, isolated from their context, may seem to be in need of rewriting. As they make complete sense when the comma is reached, the second clause has the appearance of an afterthought. Further, *and* is the least specific of connectives. Used between independent clauses, it indicates only that a relation exists between them without defining that relation. In the example above, the relation is that of cause and result. The two sentences might be rewritten:

As the early records of the city have disappeared, the story of its first years can no longer be reconstructed.

Although the situation is perilous, there is still one chance of escape.

I

ELEMENTARY RULES OF USAGE

RULE
1

RULE
2

RULE
3

RULE
4

RULE
5

RULE
6

RULE
7

或將從屬子句改寫為片語：

> Owing to the disappearance of the early records of the city, the story of its first years can no longer be reconstructed.
> 由於這座城市稍早的紀錄皆已消失，早年光景無法重建。
> In this perilous situation, there is still one chance of escape. 在這危急的情況下，仍存在一線生機。

但若讓句子過於嚴謹整齊，整篇文章可能會讀起來太正式，因此偶爾使用較鬆散的句子能給讀者一個喘息的機會。本節的第一組例句即為較鬆散的句子，常見於簡易、非學術性的文章，但學生在寫作時應避免過度使用這種句式（見規則 14）。

在兩個獨立子句合成的句子中，若第二個子句的句首為 as（因為）、for、or、nor、while（當⋯⋯），仍須在連接詞前加上逗號。

若第二個子句是以副詞開頭，則需使用分號，而非逗號（詳見規則 5）。so 和 yet 可能作副詞，也可能作連接詞用，因此第二個子句可能是並列，也可能是從屬子句，使用分號或逗號都講得通。然而我們寫作時要盡量少用 so（作 accordingly 或 so that〔因此〕解），因為

Or the subordinate clauses might be replaced by phrases:

Owing to the disappearance of the early records of
the city, the story of its first years can no longer be
reconstructed.
In this perilous situation, there is still one chance of
escape.

But a writer may err by making his sentences too uniformly
compact and periodic, and an occasional loose sentence prevents the style from becoming too formal and gives the reader
a certain relief. Consequently, loose sentences of the type first
quoted are common in easy, unstudied writing. But a writer
should be careful not to construct too many of his sentences
after this pattern (see Rule 14).

Two-part sentences of which the second member is introduced
by *as* (in the sense of *because*), *for, or, nor,* and *while* (in the
sense of *and at the same time*) likewise require a comma before the conjunction.

If the second member is introduced by an adverb, a semicolon, not a comma, is required (see Rule 5). The connectives *so*
and *yet* may be used either as adverbs or as conjunctions, accordingly as the second clause is felt to be co-ordinate or sub-

I

ELEMENTARY RULES OF
USAGE

RULE
1

RULE
2

RULE
3

RULE
4

RULE
5

RULE
6

RULE
7

這個字較不正式，建議用 as 或 since 作為第一個子句
的開頭，

例如將：

I had never been in the place before; so I had difficulty in finding my way about.

我從沒來過這裡，因此找不到路。

改為：

As I had never been in the place before, I had
difficulty in finding my way about.

我之前從沒到過這個地方，所以找不到路。

若一個從屬子句，或須以逗號隔開的引介片語後面連
接第二個獨立子句，兩個子句之間的連接詞後不須加
逗號，例如：

The situation is perilous, but if we are prepared
to act promptly, there is still one chance of escape.

儘管情況危急，但只要我們臨機應變，仍有一線生機。

ordinate; consequently either mark of punctuation may be justified. But these uses of *so* (equivalent to *accordingly* or to *so that*) are somewhat colloquial and should, as a rule, be avoided in writing. A simple correction, usually serviceable, is to omit the word *so* and begin the first clause with *as* or *since*:

> I had never been in the place before; so I had difficulty in finding my way about.
> As I had never been in the place before, I had difficulty in finding my way about.

If a dependent clause, or an introductory phrase requiring to be set off by a comma, precedes the second independent clause, no comma is needed after the conjunction.

> The situation is perilous, but if we are prepared to act promptly, there is still one chance of escape.

RULE
1

RULE
2

RULE
3

RULE
4

RULE
5

RULE
6

RULE
7

當前後兩個子句主詞相同但只寫出一次，且連接詞為 but 的時候須加逗號。若前後子句間的連接詞為 and 且兩個敘述的關係緊密或直接，則應將逗號省去。

I have heard his arguments, but am still unconvinced. 即使我聽過他的主張，仍然無法認同。
He has had several years' experience and is thoroughly competent.
他已具備好幾年的經驗，因此競爭力十足。

When the subject is the same for both clauses and is expressed only once, a comma is required if the connective is *but*. If the connective is *and*, the comma should be omitted if the relation between the two statements is close or immediate.

I have heard his arguments, but am still unconvinced.
He has had several years' experience and is thoroughly competent.

RULE
1

RULE
2

RULE
3

RULE
4

RULE
5

RULE
6

RULE
7

規則 5 不可用逗號連接獨立子句。

兩個以上文法結構完整的子句若不用連接詞連接，應該在每個字句間加入分號，形成複合句。

> Stevenson's romances are entertaining; they are full of exciting adventures.
> 史帝文森的傳奇故事趣味橫生，充滿刺激的冒險經歷。
> It is nearly half past five; we cannot reach town before dark.
> 快五點半了，我們無法在天黑之前到達鎮上。

當然也可以用句號取代分號，寫成兩個句子。

> Stevenson's romances are entertaining. They are full of exciting adventures. 史帝文森的傳奇故事趣味橫生。這些故事充滿刺激的冒險經歷。
> It is nearly half past five. We cannot reach town before dark.
> 快五點半了。我們無法在天黑之前到達鎮上。

若插入連接詞，子句間應使用逗號（見規則4），如下頁例句：

Do not join independent clauses by a comma.

If two or more clauses, grammatically complete and not joined by a conjunction, are to form a single compound sentence, the proper mark of punctuation is a semicolon.

> Stevenson's romances are entertaining; they are full of exciting adventures.
> It is nearly half past five; we cannot reach town before dark.

It is of course equally correct to write the above as two sentences each, replacing the semicolons by periods.

> Stevenson's romances are entertaining. They are full of exciting adventures.
> It is nearly half past five. We cannot reach town before dark.

If a conjunction is inserted the proper mark is a comma (see Rule 4).

RULE
1

RULE
2

RULE
3

RULE
4

RULE
5

RULE
6

RULE
7

Stevenson's romances are entertaining, for they are full of exciting adventures. 史帝文森的傳奇故事趣味橫生，因為裡頭充滿刺激的冒險經歷。

It is nearly half past five, and we cannot reach town before dark.

快五點半了，我們無法在天黑之前到達鎮上。

以上三種句型相比之下，第一種句型的優點顯而易見，至少在上面的例句中優於第二種句型，因為前者能暗示兩個敘述之間緊密的關係。第一種句型也優於第三種句型，因其較為簡潔有力。若說這種點明各敘述之間關係的方式，是最實用的寫作手法之一也不為過。

請注意，若第二個子句是以 accordingly、besides、then、therefore、thus 等副詞，而非連接詞開頭，**前後子句間仍須有分號**。

不過有兩種情況例外：子句長度很短，或前後子句句型相似時，可以用逗號連接：

Man proposes, God disposes. 謀事在人成事在天。

The gate swung apart, the bridge fell, the portcullis was drawn up.

城門打開，吊橋放下，閘門拉了上去。

> Stevenson's romances are entertaining, for they are full of exciting adventures.
> It is nearly half past five, and we cannot reach town before dark.

A comparison of the three forms given above will show clearly the advantage of the first. It is, at least in the examples given, better than the second form, because it suggests the close relationship between the two statements in a way that the second does not attempt, and better than the third, because briefer and therefore more forcible. Indeed it may be said that this simple method of indicating relationship between statements is one of the most useful devices of composition.

Note that if the second clause is preceded by an adverb, such as *accordingly*, *besides*, *then*, *therefore*, or *thus*, and not by a conjunction, the semicolon is still required.

Two exceptions to the rule may be admitted. If the clauses are very short, and are alike in form, a comma is usually permissible:

> Man proposes, God disposes.
> The gate swung apart, the bridge fell, the portcullis was drawn up.

RULE 1
RULE 2
RULE 3
RULE 4
RULE 5
RULE 6
RULE 7

請注意，在上面兩個例句中，前後子句並無因果關係。此外，在口語的表達方式中，兩個子句之間也使用逗號，而非分號，例如：

I hardly knew him, he was so changed,
他改變得太多，我都不太認得了。

但使用這種表達方式來寫作較不恰當，除非是故事或戲劇中的對話，或熟人之間的書信。

Note that in these examples the relation is not one of cause or consequence. Also in the colloquial form of expression,

I hardly knew him, he was so changed,

a comma, not a semicolon, is required. But this form of expression is inappropriate in writing, except in the dialogue of a story or play, or perhaps in a familiar letter.

RULE
1

RULE
2

RULE
3

RULE
4

RULE
5

RULE
6

RULE
7

規則6 **不可將完整句子拆成兩句。**

換句話說,不要用句號取代逗號。

（×）I met them on a Cunard liner several years ago. Coming home from Liverpool to New York.
我數年前在庫納德郵輪上認識他們,當時我正從利物浦返回家鄉紐約。

（×）He was an interesting talker. A man who had traveled all over the world and lived in half a dozen countries.
他是個有趣的講者,周遊列國並在六七個國家長住過。

在這兩個例子當中,第一個句號應該以逗號取代,並將其後的第一個字改為小寫。

若要強調某個字或措辭,則可以用句號另起一句:

Again and again he called out. No reply.
他一次又一次地呼喊,卻毫無回應。

寫作時須審慎使用強調語氣,避免被認為誤用句構或標點。

原則 3、4、5、6 為標點斷句的重要法則,寫作者必須徹底駕馭而應用自如。

RULE 6 Do not break sentences in two.

In other words, do not use periods for commas.

> (✕) I met them on a Cunard liner several years ago. Coming home from Liverpool to New York.
>
> (✕) He was an interesting talker. A man who had traveled all over the world and lived in half a dozen countries.

In both these examples, the first period should be replaced by a comma, and the following word begun with a small letter.

It is permissible to make an emphatic word or expression serve the purpose of a sentence and to punctuate it accordingly:

> Again and again he called out. No reply.

The writer must, however, be certain that the emphasis is warranted, and that he will not be suspected of a mere blunder in syntax or in punctuation.

Rules 3, 4, 5, and 6 cover the most important principles in the punctuation of ordinary sentences; they should be so thoroughly mastered that their application becomes second nature.

I

ELEMENTARY RULES OF USAGE

RULE 1

RULE 2

RULE 3

RULE 4

RULE 5

RULE 6

RULE 7

規則 1
規則 2
規則 3
規則 4
規則 5
規則 6
規則 7

規則 7　句首分詞片語所指涉的主詞，須和主要子句的主詞一致。

> Walking slowly down the road, he saw a woman accompanied by two children.
>
> 他沿著路慢慢走著，看見一名婦人帶著兩個小孩。

此句中 walking 指涉的對象是 he 而不是 woman，若要將指涉的對象改成 woman，應該將句子改寫成：

> He saw a woman, accompanied by two children, walking slowly down the road.
>
> 他看見一名婦人帶著兩個小孩，沿著路慢慢走著。

以連接詞或介系詞帶出的分詞片語、名詞同位語、形容詞和形容詞片語若位於句首，同樣適用本原則，例如：

> （×）On arriving in Chicago, his friends met him at the station.
>
> （○）When he arrived（或 On his arrival）in Chicago, his friends met him at the station.
>
> 他抵達芝加哥時，朋友在車站與他會面。

RULE 7 A participial phrase at the beginning of a sentence must refer to the grammatical subject.

Walking slowly down the road, he saw a woman accompanied by two children.

The word *walking* refers to the subject of the sentence, not to the woman. If the writer wishes to make it refer to the woman, he must recast the sentence:

He saw a woman accompanied by two children, walking slowly down the road.

Participial phrases preceded by a conjunction or by a preposition, nouns in apposition, adjectives, and adjective phrases come under the same rule if they begin the sentence.

(×) On arriving in Chicago, his friends met him at the station.
(○) When he arrived (or, On his arrival) in Chicago, his friends met him at the station.

RULE
1

RULE
2

RULE
3

RULE
4

RULE
5

RULE
6

RULE
7

（×）A soldier of proved valor, they entrusted him with the defence of the city.

（○）A solider of proved valor, he was entrusted with the defence of the city.

他是個勇敢的軍人，受託保衛城邦。

（×）Young and inexperienced, the task seemed easy to me.

（○）Young and inexperienced, I thought the task easy.

我當時年少又缺乏經驗，以為這件事易如反掌。

（×）Without a friend to counsel him, the temptation proved irresistible.

（○）Without a friend to counsel him, he found the temptation irresistible.

當時沒有朋友勸他，使他陷入誘惑、難以自拔。

違反這個原則的句子，讀起來通常不知所云，如下頁的例句：

（×）A soldier of proved valor, they entrusted him with the defence of the city.

（○）A soldier of proved valor, he was entrusted with the defence of the city.

（×）Young and inexperienced, the task seemed easy to me.

（○）Young and inexperienced, I thought the task easy.

（×）Without a friend to counsel him, the temptation proved irresistible.

（○）Without a friend to counsel him, he found the temptation irresistible.

Sentences violating this rule are often ludicrous.

RULE
1

RULE
2

RULE
3

RULE
4

RULE
5

RULE
6

RULE
7

（╳）Being in a dilapidated condition, I was able to buy the house very cheap.

在殘破不堪的情況下，我以極低廉的價格買下這棟房子。

（╳）Wondering irresolutely what to do next, the clock struck twelve.

還在對下一步猶豫不決時，時鐘敲了十二響。❺

學習小提醒 5

這兩個例句的正確用法是：

Being in a dilapidated condition, the house was bought at a low price.

Wondering irresolutely what to do next, he heard the clock struck twelve.

（×）Being in a dilapidated condition, I was able to buy the house very cheap.

（×）Wondering irresolutely what to do next, the clock struck twelve.

RULE
1

RULE
2

RULE
3

RULE
4

RULE
5

RULE
6

RULE
7

想寫出流暢、道地的句子，
你必須學會——

⊙ 用分號來合併兩個獨立子句 形成「複合句」！

⊙ 盡量少用 so，因為這個詞不夠正式、優美，你
  可以將原句改寫成以 as 或 since 開頭的句式！

⊙ 把附加說明的內容放到兩個逗號中間，注意：

  非限定關係子句 → 開頭要加上逗號；

  限定關係子句 → 開頭不可加上逗號。

⊙ 當前後子句間有因果關係時，使用 and 作為連
  接詞容易語意不清，建議用 as、although 取代！

⊙ 句首分詞片語所省略的主詞，一定要和主要子
  句的主詞一致！

英文寫作的 11 個基本原則

II

ELEMENTARY PRINCIPLES OF COMPOSITION

本章旨在鍛鍊短文寫作必備的兩大能力：
「清晰表達力＋邏輯論述力」。
請特別注意規則１３「刪除贅字」，
這是啟發無數寫作名家的經典寫作原則。

規則 8 **以段落為寫作單位，每個子題寫一段。**

若你寫作的主題內容有限，或你希望簡短言之，那可能不須再細分成數個子題。一段簡短的描述、文學作品的大綱、單一事件的前因後果、概述單一事件的敘事，或提出一個看法，都宜寫成單一段落。寫完後可再確認分段是否真的沒有幫助。

不過，寫作時通常需要將主題分成數個子題，每個子題寫成一個段落，這麼做的原因是要幫助讀者閱讀。每個新的段落都是在提醒讀者，主題已經發展到下個階段。

要分成幾段則取決於整篇文章的長度，例如一本書或一首詩的短評可以不必分段，若篇幅長一點則可以分成兩段：

A. 介紹文本內容

B. 分析與評論

RULE 8 Make the paragraph the unit of composition: one paragraph to each topic.

If the subject on which you are writing is of slight extent, or if you intend to treat it very briefly, there may be no need of subdividing it into topics. Thus a brief description, a brief summary of a literary work, a brief account of a single incident, a narrative merely outlining an action, the setting forth of a single idea, any one of these is best written in a single paragraph. After the paragraph has been written, examine it to see whether subdivision will not improve it.

Ordinarily, however, a subject requires subdivision into topics, each of which should be made the subject of a paragraph. The object of treating each topic in a paragraph by itself is, of course, to aid the reader. The beginning of each paragraph is a signal to him that a new step in the development of the subject has been reached.

The extent of subdivision will vary with the length of the composition. For example, a short notice of a book or poem might consist of a single paragraph. One slightly longer might consist of two paragraphs:

A. Account of the work.

B. Critical discussion.

RULE
8
RULE
9
RULE
10
RULE
11
RULE
12
RULE
13
RULE
14
RULE
15

在文學課上要寫一首詩的報告時，可分成七個段落：

A. 創作及出版過程

B. 詩的分類及格律

C. 詩的主題

D. 處理主題的方式

E. 寫作精采之處

F. 反映出作者風格的段落

G. 與其他作品的關聯

段落 C 和 D 的寫作方式每首詩各有不同。若有必要，段落 C 通常會指出該詩的字面內容及衍伸意象，接著說明主題及發展方式。若全詩只是以第三人稱敘述一件事情，段落 C 便只須簡短地說明大意。段落 D 則點出詩的主題及呈現的方式，抑或指出全詩強調的重點。

小說則可分為以下幾點討論：

A. 背景

B. 劇情

C. 角色

D. 目的

A report on a poem, written for a class in literature, might consist of seven paragraphs:

A. Facts of composition and publication.

B. Kind of poem; metrical form.

C. Subject.

D. Treatment of subject.

E. For what chiefly remarkable.

F. Wherein characteristic of the writer.

G. Relationship to other works.

The contents of paragraphs C and D would vary with the poem. Usually, paragraph C would indicate the actual or imagined circumstances of the poem (the situation), if these call for explanation, and would then state the subject and outline its development. If the poem is a narrative in the third person throughout, paragraph C need contain no more than a concise summary of the action. Paragraph D would indicate the leading ideas and show how they are made prominent, or would indicate what points in the narrative are chiefly emphasized.

A novel might be discussed under the heads:

A. Setting.

B. Plot.

C. Characters.

D. Purpose.

II

ELEMENTARY PRINCIPLES OF COMPOSITION

RULE 8

RULE 9

RULE 10

RULE 11

RULE 12

RULE 13

RULE 14

RULE 15

歷史事件可分為以下幾點討論：

A. 起因

B. 經過

C. 影響與後續

在探討這兩類主題時，同學可能會發現，有些子題需要分段書寫。

請注意不要把一個句子當作一段，除非那個句子有連接的功能，能指出前後論點或段落間的關係。教科書、手冊和其他以較簡短方式說明主題的文本亦不在此限。

在對話中，每段發言（就算只有一個字）都是一個段落，亦即每次換人說話就是一個新段落的開始。那當對話和敘事結合時如何應用這個原則呢？參考暢銷小說中的例子是最好的方式。

An historical event might be discussed under the heads:

A. What led up to the event.

B. Account of the event.

C. What the event led up to.

In treating either of these last two subjects, the writer would probably find it necessary to subdivide one or more of the topics here given.

As a rule, single sentences should not be written or printed as paragraphs. An exception may be made of sentences of transition, indicating the relation between the parts of an exposition or argument. Frequent exceptions are also necessary in textbooks, guidebooks, and other works in which many topics are treated briefly.

In dialogue, each speech, even if only a single word, is a paragraph by itself; that is, a new paragraph begins with each change of speaker. The application of this rule, when dialogue and narrative are combined, is best learned from examples in well-printed works of fiction.

RULE
8

RULE
9

RULE
10

RULE
11

RULE
12

RULE
13

RULE
14

RULE
15

規則 **9** 每個段落以一句主題句 (topic sentence)
開頭，結尾須與開頭呼應。

本原則的目的同樣是幫助讀者閱讀，這種寫作方式能
讓讀者在開始閱讀每個段落時，就掌握該段落的目
的，且直到段落結束時都銘記在心。因此，在闡釋或
議論時最常使用的段落結構為：

(a) 主題句在首句或前幾句出現；

(b) 接下來的句子解釋、建立或發展主題句的敘述；

(c) 末句強調主題句的想法，或陳述一些重要結論。

請避免以離題的敘述，或無關緊要的細節作為段落的
結尾。

若文章的篇幅較長，寫作時可能必須說明某個段落與
前述內容的關聯，或該段落在通篇文章中的功能。有
時只須在主題句中加入一個詞語，如 again（同樣地）、
therefore（因此）、for the same reason（由於同樣的原因），
有時則須在主題句前加上一或數句有引導或連接功能
的句子。若需要多個句子才能與主題句順利銜接，則
建議將這幾個句子獨立為一個段落。

RULE 9   As a rule, begin each paragraph with a topic sentence, end it in conformity with the beginning.

Again, the object is to aid the reader. The practice here recommended enables him to discover the purpose of each paragraph as he begins to read it, and to retain this purpose in mind as he ends it. For this reason, the most generally useful kind of paragraph, particularly in exposition and argument, is that in which

(a) the topic sentence comes at or near the beginning;

(b) the succeeding sentences explain or establish or develop the statement made in the topic sentence; and

(c) the final sentence either emphasizes the thought of the topic sentence or states some important consequence.

Ending with a digression, or with an unimportant detail, is particularly to be avoided.

If the paragraph forms part of a larger composition, its relation to what precedes, or its function as a part of the whole, may need to be expressed. This can sometimes be done by a mere word or phrase (*again*; *therefore*; *for the same reason*) in the topic sentence. Sometimes, however, it is expedient to precede the topic sentence by one or more sentences of introduction or transition. If more than one such sentence is required, it is

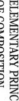

II

ELEMENTARY PRINCIPLES
OF COMPOSITION

RULE
8

RULE
9

RULE
10

RULE
11

RULE
12

RULE
13

RULE
14

RULE
15

如上所述，同學在寫作時可以運用數種方式連結段落中的本文與主題句。你／妳也可以用不同的句式重述主題句、定義句中的詞彙、反駁與主題句相反的事實、提供通例或特例、說明句子的隱含意義或其可能導致的結果，來讓主題句要表達的意義更加明確。在寫作較長的段落時，同學可能會用到以上數種方法。

範例1 **蘇格蘭小說家史蒂文森的經典散文〈徒步旅行〉**

❶主題句。

Now, to be properly enjoyed, a walking tour should be gone upon alone.

若要好好享受徒步旅行，你應該自己一個人去。

❷否定相反的做法以闡明主旨。

If you go in a company, or even in pairs, it is no longer a walking tour in anything but name; it is something else and more in the nature of a picnic.

如果是一群人去，或就算只有兩個人，也只會是趟有名無實的徒步旅行；比起徒步旅行，這更像是去野餐。

generally better to set apart the transitional sentences as a separate paragraph.

According to the writer's purpose, he may, as indicated above, relate the body of the paragraph to the topic sentence in one or more of several different ways. He may make the meaning of the topic sentence clearer by restating it in other forms, by defining its terms, by denying the contrary, by giving illustrations or specific instances; he may establish it by proofs; or he may develop it by showing its implications and consequences. In a long paragraph, he may carry out several of these processes.

Example 1 Robert Louis Stevenson, *Walking Tour*

❶ Topic sentence.
Now, to be properly enjoyed, a walking tour should be gone upon alone.

❷ The meaning made clearer by denial of the contrary.
If you go in a company, or even in pairs, it is no longer a walking tour in anything but name; it is something else and more in the nature of a picnic.

II

ELEMENTARY PRINCIPLES OF COMPOSITION

RULE
8

RULE
9

RULE
10

RULE
11

RULE
12

RULE
13

RULE
14

RULE
15

❸以簡短的方式重述主題句,並提出三個原因支持;其中,第三個原因(「你必須擁有自己的步調」)是用反駁與主題句相反的事實的方式,來闡明意見。

A walking tour should be gone upon alone, because freedom is of the essence; because you should be able to stop and go on, and follow this way or that, as the freak takes you; and because you must have your own pace, and neither trot alongside a champion walker, nor mince in time with a girl. 徒步旅行應該自己一個人去,因為自由是其中的精髓;因為如此一來,你便能隨時走走停停,或隨興改變路徑;因為你必須擁有自己的步調,而不是在一位快走冠軍旁小跑步,或因為一位女孩而停駐許久。

❹用兩種方式敘述第四個原因。

And you must be open to all impressions and let your thoughts take colour from what you see.
你也應該敞開心胸接受任何映入眼簾的印象,並讓所見之物為你的想法增色。

❺用另一種方式敘述同一個原因。

You should be as a pipe for any wind to play upon.
你該像把笛子,不管什麼風吹來,都能奏出美妙樂音。

❸ The topic sentence repeated, in abridged form, and supported by three reasons; the meaning of the third ("you must have your own pace") made clearer by denying the contrary.

A walking tour should be gone upon alone, because freedom is of the essence; because you should be able to stop and go on, and follow this way or that, as the freak takes you; and because you must have your own pace, and neither trot alongside a champion walker, nor mince in time with a girl.

❹ A fourth reason, stated in two forms.

And you must be open to all impressions and let your thoughts take colour from what you see.

❺ The same reason, stated in still another form.

You should be as a pipe for any wind to play upon.

RULE
8

RULE
9

RULE
10

RULE
11

RULE
12

RULE
13

RULE
14

RULE
15

❻引述英國散文家 Hazlitt 的話說明同一個原因。

"I cannot see the wit," says Hazlitt, "of walking and talking at the same time. When I am in the country, I wish to vegetate like the country," which is the gist of all that can be said upon the matter. 海茲利特說道:「我看不出邊散步邊講話的好處。當我走在鄉間時,我只想像植物般悠然生長。」這段話說得實在中肯。

❼將 Hazlitt 的話換句話說。

There should be no cackle of voices at your elbow, to jar on the meditative silence of the morning. 你身邊不該有呶呶不休的人聲,破壞早晨冥想般的寧靜。

❽以豐富、生動的用詞再次重述第四個原因,形成強而有力的結論。

And so long as a man is reasoning he cannot surrender himself to that fine intoxication that comes of much motion in the open air, that begins in a sort of dazzle and sluggishness of the brain, and ends in a peace that passes comprehension.
而且當一個人用理性思考時,他便無法美好地沉醉在自然之中,這種沉醉來自空氣中的律動,源於大腦的微醺與慵懶,並在一種難以名狀的平靜之中落幕。

❻ The same reason as stated by Hazlitt.

"I cannot see the wit," says Hazlitt, "of walking and talking at the same time. When I am in the country, I wish to vegetate like the country," which is the gist of all that can be said upon the matter.

❼ Repetition, in paraphrase, of the quotation from Hazlitt.

There should be no cackle of voices at your elbow, to jar on the meditative silence of the morning.

❽ Final statement of the fourth reason, in language amplified and heightened to form a strong conclusion.

And so long as a man is reasoning he cannot surrender himself to that fine intoxication that comes of much motion in the open air, that begins in a sort of dazzle and sluggishness of the brain, and ends in a peace that passes comprehension.

RULE
8

RULE
9

RULE
10

RULE
11

RULE
12

RULE
13

RULE
14

RULE
15

範例 2 **愛爾蘭政治理論家李克〈歷史的政治價值〉**

❶主題句。

It was chiefly in the eighteenth century that a very different conception of history grew up.
在十八世紀，一種十分不同的史觀逐漸興起。

❷解釋主題句的意義；定義歷史的新概念。

Historians then came to believe that their task was not so much to paint a picture as to solve a problem; to explain or illustrate the successive phases of national growth, prosperity, and adversity. 史學家開始相信他們的任務並非描摹過去，而是解決問題，並為國家成長、繁榮或消亡的每個階段舉例說明、詳加解釋。

規則 8
規則 9
規則 10
規則 11
規則 12
規則 13
規則 14
規則 15

Example 2 Lecky, *The Political Value of History*

❶ Topic sentence.
It was chiefly in the eighteenth century that a very different conception of history grew up.

❷ The meaning of the topic sentence made clearer; the new conception of history defined.
Historians then came to believe that their task was not so much to paint a picture as to solve a problem; to explain or illustrate the successive phases of national growth, prosperity, and adversity.

RULE
8

RULE
9

RULE
10

RULE
11

RULE
12

RULE
13

RULE
14

RULE
15

❸擴展前述的定義。

The history of morals, of industry, of intellect, and of art; the changes that take place in manners or beliefs; the dominant ideas that prevailed in successive periods; the rise, fall, and modification of political constitutions; in a word, all the conditions of national well-being became the subject of their works. 道德、產業、知識和藝術的歷史；禮儀或信仰上的改變；每個時期的主流思想；政治結構的興衰與更替……總而言之，與國勢相關的任何條件都可能是他們書寫的主題。

❹以反面解釋定義。

They sought rather to write a history of peoples than a history of kings. 他們寧願書寫市井小民的歷史，而非王公貴族的歷史。

❺提出歷史新概念中的另一個細節，以補充說明定義。

They looked especially in history for the chain of causes and effects.
他們也特別留意歷史中的因果鏈。

❸ The definition expanded.

The history of morals, of industry, of intellect, and of art; the changes that take place in manners or beliefs; the dominant ideas that prevailed in successive periods; the rise, fall, and modification of political constitutions; in a word, all the conditions of national well-being became the subject of their works.

❹ The definition explained by contrast.

They sought rather to write a history of peoples than a history of kings.

❺ The definition supplemented: another element in the new conception of history.

They looked especially in history for the chain of causes and effects.

RULE
8

RULE
9

RULE
10

RULE
11

RULE
12

RULE
13

RULE
14

RULE
15

❻結論：歷史新概念導致的重要結果。

They undertook to study in the past the physiology of nations, and hoped by applying the experimental method on a large scale to deduce some
lessons of real value about the conditions on
which the welfare of society mainly depend.

他們扛下責任，研究一個國家過去的生理狀況，並期望藉
由大量套用實驗方法，得出一些有價值的教訓，是締造社
會福祉的一大要素。

敘事型和描述型的段落，通常會用簡短、概括性的句
子開頭，來連結後續的細節，例如：

The breeze served us admirably. 微風吹得正好。
The campaign opened with a series of reverses.
抗議活動一開始即屢遭挫敗。
The next ten or twelve pages were filled with a
curious set of entries.
接下來的十多頁充滿了許多有趣的條目。

❻ Conclusion: an important consequence of the new conception of history.

They undertook to study in the past the physiology of nations, and hoped by applying the experimental method on a large scale to deduce some lessons of real value about the conditions on which the welfare of society mainly depend.

In narration and description the paragraph sometimes begins with a concise, comprehensive statement serving to hold together the details that follow.

The breeze served us admirably.
The campaign opened with a series of reverses.
The next ten or twelve pages were filled with a curious set of entries.

II

ELEMENTARY PRINCIPLES
OF COMPOSITION

RULE
8

RULE
9

RULE
10

RULE
11

RULE
12

RULE
13

RULE
14

RULE
15

若過度使用這種寫法，讀起來會很像在套公式。較常見的做法仍是以起始句說明段落主要探討的內容。

> At length I thought I might return towards the stockade. 最後我覺得自己會回到城寨去。
> He picked up the heavy lamp from the table and began to explore.
> 他拿起桌上沉重的檯燈，開始四處探索。
> Another flight of steps, and they emerged on the roof. 他們又爬了一層樓的階梯，隨即出現在屋頂上。

強調動態感的簡短段落則通常沒有主題句，分段本身即在修辭上達到停頓的效果，也強調了情節中的某些細節。

規則 8

規則 9

規則 10

規則 11

規則 12

規則 13

規則 14

規則 15

But this device, if too often used, would become a mannerism. More commonly the opening sentence simply indicates by its subject with what the paragraph is to be principally concerned.

> At length I thought I might return towards the stockade.
> He picked up the heavy lamp from the table and began to explore.
> Another flight of steps, and they emerged on the roof.

The brief paragraphs of animated narrative, however, are often without even this semblance of a topic sentence. The break between them serves the purpose of a rhetorical pause, throwing into prominence some detail of the action.

RULE
8

RULE
9

RULE
10

RULE
11

RULE
12

RULE
13

RULE
14

RULE
15

規則 10 使用主動語態。

主動語態通常比被動語態更自然有力，例如：

> I shall always remember my first visit to Boston.
> 我會永遠記得生平第一趟波士頓之旅。

寫成被動則是：

> My first visit to Boston will always be remembered by me. 生平第一趟波士頓之旅會永遠被我記得。

第二個句子顯得迂迴、無力而冗長。若想讓句子更簡潔而把 by me 去掉，寫成

> My first visit to Boston will always be remembered. 我生平第一趟波士頓之旅會永遠被銘記在心。

則會顯得語意不清：是作者本人、某個未知的人物，還是世上的眾人都會記得那趟旅程呢？
當然這並不表示寫作時要完全捨棄被動語態；它仍相當實用，且某些狀況下必須使用被動。

RULE 10 Use the active voice.

The active voice is usually more direct and vigorous than the passive:

> I shall always remember my first visit to Boston.

This is much better than

> My first visit to Boston will always be remembered by me.

The latter sentence is less direct, less bold, and less concise. If the writer tries to make it more concise by omitting "by me,"

> My first visit to Boston will always be remembered.

it becomes indefinite: is it the writer, or some person undisclosed, or the world at large, that will always remember this visit?

This rule does not, of course, mean that the writer should entirely discard the passive voice, which is frequently convenient and sometimes necessary.

II

ELEMENTARY PRINCIPLES
OF COMPOSITION

RULE
8

RULE
9

RULE
10

RULE
11

RULE
12

RULE
13

RULE
14

RULE
15

The dramatists of the Restoration are little es-
teemed to-day. 復辟時期的劇作家如今鮮少受人尊敬。
Modern readers have little esteem or the drama-
tist of the Restoration.
現在的讀者甚少尊敬復辟時期的劇作家。

第一個句子應該會出現在以復辟時期劇作家為主題的
段落中，第二個句子則會出現在描述現代人閱讀品味
的段落中。如例句所示，主詞的選擇便會決定語態的
使用。

此外，不要堆疊被動語態。

（×）Gold was not allowed to be exported.

（○）It was forbidden to export gold.

（○）The export of gold was prohibited.

當時不允許出口黃金。

（×）He has been proved to have been seen en-
tering the building.

（○）It has been proved that he was seen to en-
ter the building.

有人看見他進入建築物一事已被證實。

> The dramatists of the Restoration are little esteemed to-day.
>
> Modern readers have little esteem for the dramatists of the Restoration.

The first would be the right form in a paragraph on the dramatists of the Restoration; the second, in a paragraph on the tastes of modern readers. The need of making a particular word the subject of the sentence will often, as in these examples, determine which voice is to be used.

As a rule, avoid making one passive depend directly upon another.

> (×) Gold was not allowed to be exported.
> (○) It was forbidden to export gold.
> (○) The export of gold was prohibited.

> (×) He has been proved to have been seen entering the building.
> (○) It has been proved that he was seen to enter the building.

RULE
8

RULE
9

RULE
10

RULE
11

RULE
12

RULE
13

RULE
14

RULE
15

在兩個未修改的句子中，gold 和 he 原本應與第二個
被動動詞 export 和 see 相關，卻被當作第一個被動動
詞 allow 和 prove 的主詞。

另一個常見錯誤則是將原本敘述動作的字詞（如下列
第一句中的 survey）當作被動語態的主詞，使得後頭
必須搪塞毫無意義的動詞❶。

（×）A survey of this region was <u>made</u> in 1900.

（○）The region was surveyed in 1900.

曾有人在 1900 年調查這個區域。

（×）Mobilization of the army was rapidly <u>effect-
ed</u>.

（○）The army was rapidly mobilized.

軍隊迅速地動員。

（×）Confirmation of these reports cannot be
<u>obtained</u>.

（○）These reports cannot be confirmed.

這些報導的虛實無法確認。

學習小提醒 1

第一句的 made、第二句的 effected、第三句的 obtained 是毫無意義的動詞，
這些字詞除了完成句子外，沒有其他功能。

In both the examples above, before correction, the word properly related to the second passive is made the subject of the first.

A common fault is to use as the subject of a passive construction a noun which expresses the entire action, leaving to the verb no function beyond that of completing the sentence.

(✕) A survey of this region was made in 1900.
(◯) This region was surveyed in 1900.

(✕) Mobilization of the army was rapidly effected.
(◯) The army was rapidly mobilized.

(✕) Confirmation of these reports cannot be obtained.
(◯) These reports cannot be confirmed.

II

ELEMENTARY PRINCIPLES
OF COMPOSITION

RULE
8

RULE
9

RULE
10

RULE
11

RULE
12

RULE
13

RULE
14

RULE
15

寫作者可以比較上述例子的第一句，和第76頁的「The export of gold was prohibited」，其中的述語 was prohibited 和 export 所表達的意義沒有重複。

經常使用主動語態能讓寫作有力許多，這並不限於以描述動作為主的敘事，而適用於各種文類。只要用主動語態的動詞取代一些平凡的用詞（如 there is 或 could be heard），許多乏味的描述或議論就能生動有力許多，例如：

（×）There were a great number of dead leaves lying on the ground.

（○）Dead leaves covered the ground.

枯葉覆蓋了地面。

（×）The sound of a guitar somewhere in the house could be heard.

（○）Somewhere in the house the guitar hummed sleepily.

房子的某處傳來了朦朧的吉他聲。

Compare the sentence, "The export of gold was prohibited," in which the predicate "was prohibited" expresses something not implied in "export."

The habitual use of the active voice makes for forcible writing. This is true not only in narrative principally concerned with action, but in writing of any kind. Many a tame sentence of description or exposition can be made lively and emphatic by substituting a verb in the active voice for some such perfunctory expression as *there is*, or *could be heard*.

(✗) There were a great number of dead leaves lying on the ground.

(○) Dead leaves covered the ground.

(✗) The sound of a guitar somewhere in the house could be heard.

(○) Somewhere in the house a guitar hummed sleepily.

RULE
8

RULE
9

RULE
10

RULE
11

RULE
12

RULE
13

RULE
14

RULE
15

（×）The reason that he left college was that his health became impaired.

（○）Falling health compelled him to leave college.

健康狀況不佳使他不得不離開了大學。

（×）It was not long before he was very sorry that he had said what he had.

（○）He soon repented his words.

他隨即對自己說的話感到懊悔。

(×) The reason that he left college was that his health became impaired.

(○) Failing health compelled him to leave college.

(×) It was not long before he was very sorry that he had said what he had.

(○) He soon repented his words.

II

ELEMENTARY PRINCIPLES OF COMPOSITION

RULE
8

RULE
9

RULE
10

RULE
11

RULE
12

RULE
13

RULE
14

RULE
15

規則 11　盡量使用肯定句。

提出論點時語意要明確，避免使用平淡無力、模稜兩可的字詞。Not 應該只用在表達否定或對比修辭時，不要用來規避正面論述，例如：

（×）*The Taming of the Shrew* is rather weak in spots. Shakespeare does not portray Katharine as a very admirable character, nor does Bianca remain long in memory as an important character in Shakespeare's works.

（○）The women in *The Taming of the Shrew* are unattractive. Katharine is disagreeable, Bianca insignificant.

《馴悍記》中的女性角色缺乏魅力，凱瑟琳不甚討喜，畢安卡更無足輕重。

（×）He did not think that studying Latin was much use.

（○）He thought the study of Latin useless.

他覺得研究拉丁文沒什麼用。

RULE 11 Put statements in positive form.

Make definite assertions. Avoid tame, colorless, hesitating, non-committal language. Use the word *not* as a means of denial or in antithesis, never as a means of evasion.

(✗) *The Taming of the Shrew* is rather weak in spots. Shakespeare does not portray Katharine as a very admirable character, nor does Bianca remain long in memory as an important character in Shakespeare's works.

(○) The women in *The Taming of the Shrew* are unattractive. Katharine is disagreeable, Bianca insignificant.

(✗) He did not think that studying Latin was much use.
(○) He thought the study of Latin useless.

II

ELEMENTARY PRINCIPLES OF COMPOSITION

RULE 8

RULE 9

RULE 10

RULE 11

RULE 12

RULE 13

RULE 14

RULE 15

（×）He was not very often on time.

（○）He usually came late.

他常常遲到。

在第一個例子中，第一個句子不僅語意不明確，還帶給讀者負面的感受；修正後的版本能簡潔明確地猜測作者的意圖。

上述三個例子都說明了 not 這個詞的弱點，**不管在何種情況下，讀者讀到「A 不是 B」時都不會滿意；他們想知道「A 是什麼」**。因此請謹記在心，表達否定語意時，使用肯定句仍是個較好的選擇，例如：

not honest → dishonest 不誠實

not important → trifling 瑣碎的

did not remember → forgot 忘記

did not pay any attention to → ignored 忽略

did not have much confidence in → distrusted
不信任

(✕) He was not very often on time.
(◯) He usually came late.

The first example, before correction, is indefinite as well as negative. The corrected version, consequently, is simply a guess at the writer's intention.

All three examples show the weakness inherent in the word *not*. Consciously or unconsciously, the reader is dissatisfied with being told only what is not; he wishes to be told what is. Hence, as a rule, it is better to express even a negative in positive form.

not honest → dishonest
not important → trifling
did not remember → forgot
did not pay any attention to → ignored
did not have much confidence in → distrusted

RULE
8

RULE
9

RULE
10

RULE
11

RULE
12

RULE
13

RULE
14

RULE
15

將否定句和肯定句並置（對比修辭）通常強而有力：

Not charity, but simple justice.

這並不是救濟，而是簡單的正義。

Not that I loved Caesar less, but Rome the more.

我愛凱撒，更愛羅馬。

除 not 之外的否定詞語氣通常也較強，例如：

The sun never sets upon the British flag.

大不列顛，日不落國。

The antithesis of negative and positive is strong:

> Not charity, but simple justice.
>
> Not that I loved Caesar less, but Rome the more.

Negative words other than *not* are usually strong:

> The sun never sets upon the British flag.

II

ELEMENTARY PRINCIPLES
OF COMPOSITION

RULE
8

RULE
9

RULE
10

RULE
11

RULE
12

RULE
13

RULE
14

RULE
15

規則 12 選擇語意清楚、明確的用詞。

選用精準、明確、具體,而非概括、模糊、抽象的詞語。

（×）A period of unfavorable weather set in.
來了段愁眉不展的天氣。

（〇）It rained every day for a week.
雨下了一個禮拜都沒停。

（×）He showed satisfaction as he took possession of his well-earned reward.
當他拿到取之有道的報酬時,臉上露出了滿意之情。

（〇）He grinned as he pocketed the coin.
他把金幣收進口袋裡,咧嘴笑著。

（×）There is a general agreement among those who have enjoyed the experience that surf-riding is productive of great exhilaration. 那些享受過衝浪的人一致認同,衝浪能製造許多興奮情緒。

（〇）All who have tried surf-riding agree that it is most exhilarating. 衝過浪的人都覺得實在很刺激。

RULE 12 Use definite, specific, concrete language.

Prefer the specific to the general, the definite to the vague, the concrete to the abstract.

(✗) A period of unfavorable weather set in.

(○) It rained every day for a week.

(✗) He showed satisfaction as he took possession of his well-earned reward.

(○) He grinned as he pocketed the coin.

(✗) There is a general agreement among those who have enjoyed the experience that surf-riding is productive of great exhilaration.

(○) All who have tried surf-riding agree that it is most exhilarating.

II

ELEMENTARY PRINCIPLES
OF COMPOSITION

RULE
8

RULE
9

RULE
10

RULE
11

RULE
12

RULE
13

RULE
14

RULE
15

激起讀者好奇心、使其手不釋卷的關鍵，在於使用精準、明確而具體的詞語：這個原則可能是研究寫作的各路英雄一致認同的一點。文學評論家指出最傑出的作家——荷馬、但丁、莎士比亞都以貼切而明確用語著稱，名留青史。英國詩人白朗寧（Robert Browning）則是一個較近代的例子，寫過許多精采的文句，以下節錄〈我的前公爵夫人〉裡的詩句：

> 先生，她始終如一呢！胸口佩戴著
> 我的餽贈或落日的餘光
> 或一段太殷勤的那廝
> 在果園裡折給她的櫻桃枝，或她騎著
> 繞著花圃的白騾，這一切
> 都會讓她贊羨不絕
> 或至少漲紅了臉

以及全詩的最後幾行：

> 瞅一眼海神尼普敦吧，
> 他正馴著一隻海馬，這是件珍貴的
> 收藏品。是名匠克勞斯為我鑄銅，
> 親身打造。

這些文字喚起了許多畫面。

If those who have studied the art of writing are in accord on any one point, it is on this, that the surest method of arousing and holding the attention of the reader is by being specific, definite, and concrete. Critics have pointed out how much of the effectiveness of the greatest writers, Homer, Dante, Shakespeare, results from their constant definiteness and concreteness. Browning, to cite a more modern author, affords many striking examples. Take, for instance, the lines from *My Last Duchess*,

> Sir, 'twas all one! My favour at her breast,
> The dropping of the daylight in the west,
> The bough of cherries some officious fool
> Broke in the orchard for her, the white mule
> She rode with round the terrace—all and each
> Would draw from her alike the approving speech,
> Or blush, at least,

and those which end the poem,

> Notice Neptune, though,
> Taming a sea-horse, thought a rarity,
> Which Claus of Innsbruck cast in bronze for me.

These words call up pictures.

II

ELEMENTARY PRINCIPLES
OF COMPOSITION

RULE
8

RULE
9

RULE
10

RULE
11

RULE
12

RULE
13

RULE
14

RULE
15

敘事和描寫類的散文也能用同樣的方式寫得生動。如果吉姆 (Jim Hawkins) 和大衛・巴爾福 (David Balfour)、金 (Kim)、諾斯托莫 (Nostromo) 這些冒險小說主角的經驗能讓無數的讀者身歷其境；如果在閱讀卡萊爾 (Thomas Carlyle) 的作品時，我們幾乎能感受到攻陷巴士底監獄的激情，便是因為作者使用了具體的詞彙，精準地描述了其中細節。作者不可能也沒必要呈現每一個細節；重點在於用精確的詞語描繪有意義的細節，而非模糊帶過。此外，**選用的詞彙也要夠具象，才能啟動讀者的想像力，讓他們將自己投射到畫面之中。**

在說明或論述時，同學也必須遵循「具體原則」。就算主題較大，也必須提出明確的例證：

「用詞精確的優勢在於，把文字轉換成想法需要氣力，而我們在思考時運用的是精確的概念，而非概括性的——不管要指涉的是哪個類別的事物，我們都是以類別中的個體來進行聯想，因此若我們使用了一個抽象的字，聽者或讀者就必須從諸多意象中選擇一個和多個相符的，才能會意。在這個過程中必會花費額外的時間或氣力。因此，若我們能使用一個精準的詞

Prose, in particular narrative and descriptive prose, is made vivid by the same means. If the experiences of Jim Hawkins and of David Balfour, of Kim, of Nostromo, have seemed for the moment real to countless readers, if in reading Carlyle we have almost the sense of being physically present at the taking of the Bastille, it is because of the definiteness of the details and the concreteness of the terms used. It is not that every detail is given; that would be impossible, as well as to no purpose; but that all the significant details are given, and not vaguely, but with such definiteness that the reader, in imagination, can project himself into the scene.

In exposition and in argument, the writer must likewise never lose his hold upon the concrete, and even when he is dealing with general principles, he must give particular instances of their application.

"This superiority of specific expressions is clearly due to the effort required to translate words into thoughts. As we do not think in generals, but in particulars—as whenever any class of things is referred to, we represent it to ourselves by calling to mind individual members of it, it follows that when an abstract word is used, the hearer or reader has to choose, from his stock of images, one or more by which he may figure to

RULE
8

RULE
9

RULE
10

RULE
11

RULE
12

RULE
13

RULE
14

RULE
15

彙，便能立刻喚起某個特定的意象，既省時、又省力，更能製造出生動的印象。」

上述段落引自赫伯特·斯賓塞 (Herbert Spencer) 的《款色哲學》(*The Philosophy of Style*)，他更用以下的例子來說明這個寫作原則：

（×）In proportion as the manners, customs, and amusements of a nation are cruel and bar-barous, the regulations of their penal code will be severe. 若一個國家的禮儀、習俗和娛樂殘忍又野蠻，其刑罰想必也會相當嚴苛。

（○）In proportion as men delight in battles, bull-fights, and combats of gladiators, will they punish by hanging, burning, and the rack.
如果人們能在戰爭、鬥牛和角鬥士決鬥中得到快樂，他們必會以絞刑、火刑或肢刑來處罰他人。

himself the genus mentioned. In doing this, some delay must arise, some force be expended; and if by employing a specific term an appropriate image can be at once suggested, an economy is achieved, and a more vivid impression produced."

Herbert Spencer, from whose *Philosophy of Style* the preceding paragraph is quoted, illustrates the principle by the sentences:

(×) In proportion as the manners, customs, and amusements of a nation are cruel and barbarous, the regulations of their penal code will be severe.
(○) In proportion as men delight in battles, bullfights, and combats of gladiators, will they punish by hanging, burning, and the rack.

RULE
8

RULE
9

RULE
10

RULE
11

RULE
12

RULE
13

RULE
14

RULE
15

規則 **13** 刪除贅字。

文章要簡潔才有力。句子裡不該有冗詞，段落裡也不該有冗句。但這並不代表每個句子都要寫得很短，或寫作時要省略所有細節只寫綱要，而是要「字字有真意」。

左邊的常見用語都違反了這個原則，建議修改為右邊：

the question as to whether	whether (the question whether) 是否
there is no doubt but that	no doubt (doubtless) 無疑
used for fuel purposes	used for fuel 當作燃料
he is a man who	he 他
in a hasty manner	hastily 迅速地
this is a subject which	this subject 這個主題
His story is a strange one	His story is strange 他的故事很不尋常
the reason why is that	because 因為

RULE 13 Omit needless words.

Vigorous writing is concise. A sentence should contain no unnecessary words, a paragraph no unnecessary sentences. This requires not that the writer make all his sentences short, or that he avoid all detail and treat his subjects only in outline, but that he make every word tell.

Many expressions in common use violate this principle:

the question as to whether	whether (the question whether)
there is no doubt but that	no doubt (doubtless)
used for fuel purposes	used for fuel
he is a man who	he
in a hasty manner	hastily
this is a subject which	this subject
His story is a strange one	His story is strange
the reason why is that	because

II

ELEMENTARY PRINCIPLES OF COMPOSITION

RULE
8

RULE
9

RULE
10

RULE
11

RULE
12

RULE
13

RULE
14

RULE
15

特別注意，the fact that 不管出現在何處都是冗詞，必須改寫：

待修用法	建議用法
owing to the fact that	since (because) 因為
in spite of the fact that	though (although) 儘管
call your attention to the fact that	remind you (notify you) 提醒你
I was unaware of the fact that	I was unaware that (did not know) 我不知道
the fact that he had not succeeded	his failure 他的失敗
the fact that I had arrived	my arrival 我的到來

其他需注意的用詞如 case、character、nature、system 請參照第四章。Who is、which was 之輩也常是冗詞。

待修用法	建議用法
His brother, who is a member of the same firm.	His brother, a member of the same firm. 他在同一家公司上班的哥哥
Trafalgar, which was Nelson's last battle.	Trafalgar, Nelson's last battle. 尼爾森打的最後一場仗——特拉法加海戰

In especial the expression *the fact that* should be revised out of every sentence in which it occurs.

owing to the fact that	since (because)
in spite of the fact that	though (although)
call your attention to the fact that	remind you (notify you)
I was unaware of the fact that	I was unaware that (did not know)
the fact that he had not succeeded	his failure
the fact that I had arrived	my arrival

See also under *case*, *character*, *nature*, *system* in Chapter IV.

Who is, *which was*, and the like are often superfluous.

owing to the fact that	since (because)
His brother, who is a member of the same firm.	His brother, a member of the same firm.
Trafalgar, which was Nelson's last battle.	Trafalgar, Nelson's last battle.

II

ELEMENTARY PRINCIPLES OF COMPOSITION

RULE
8

RULE
9

RULE
10

RULE
11

RULE
12

RULE
13

RULE
14

RULE
15

肯定敘述比否定來得簡潔；主動語態比被動來得簡潔，規則 11 和 12 中的許多例子也能為本原則佐證。另有一種常見的寫法違反簡潔原則——把一個較複雜的概念以一系列的句子或獨立子句逐步說明。將所有句子合併為一句會是更好的做法。

原文	建議寫法
Macbeth was very ambitious. This led him to wish to become king of Scotland. The witches told him that this wish of his would come true. The king of Scotland at this time was Duncan. Encouraged by his wife, Macbeth murdered Duncan. He was thus enabled to succeed Duncan as king. (51 words.) 馬克白野心勃勃。這讓他想成為蘇格蘭的國王。女巫們告訴他願望會成真。當時的蘇格蘭國王是鄧肯。馬克白在妻子的慫恿下謀殺了鄧肯。他因此能夠繼承王位。（51字）	Encouraged by his wife, Macbeth achieved his ambition and realized the prediction of the witches by murdering Duncan and becoming king of Scotland in his place. (26 words.) 在妻子的慫恿之下，馬克白謀殺了鄧肯，繼承了蘇格蘭的王位。他成就了自己的野心，也應驗了女巫們的預言。（26字）

As positive statement is more concise than negative, and the active voice more concise than the passive, many of the examples given under Rules 11 and 12 illustrate this rule as well.

A common violation of conciseness is the presentation of a single complex idea, step by step, in a series of sentences or independent clauses which might to advantage be combined into one.

Macbeth was very ambitious. This led him to wish to become king of Scotland. The witches told him that this wish of his would come true. The king of Scotland at this time was Duncan. Encouraged by his wife, Macbeth murdered Duncan. He was thus enabled to succeed Duncan as king. (51 words.)	Encouraged by his wife, Macbeth achieved his ambition and realized the prediction of the witches by murdering Duncan and becoming king of Scotland in his place. (26 words.)

II

ELEMENTARY PRINCIPLES OF COMPOSITION

RULE 8
RULE 9
RULE 10
RULE 11
RULE 12
RULE 13
RULE 14
RULE 15

原文	建議寫法
There were several less important courses, but these were the most important, and although they did not come every day, they came often enough to keep you in such a state of mind that you never knew what your next move would be. (43 words.) 即使有些較無關緊要的課程，這些課是最重要的，而就算沒有每天接觸，也足夠讓一個人拿不定下一步該怎麼走。（43字）	These, the most important courses of all, came, if not daily, at least often enough to keep one under constant strain. (21 words.) 那些最重要的課程，就算沒有每天接觸，也足夠讓一個人倍感壓力。（21字）

| There were several less important courses, but these were the most important, and although they did not come every day, they came often enough to keep you in such a state of mind that you never knew what your next move would be. (43 words.) | These, the most important courses of all, came, if not daily, at least often enough to keep one under constant strain. (21 words.) |

RULE
8

RULE
9

RULE
10

RULE
11

RULE
12

RULE
13

RULE
14

RULE
15

規則14 避免使用一連串結構鬆散的句子。

這個原則適用於以下這種特定的句構：句中包含兩個對等子句，其中第二個子句以連接詞或關係代名詞開頭。這種句構單獨看來相當實用（見規則 4），但連用幾次便會讓文章讀來生硬無趣。

寫作技巧欠佳的作者可能會用這種句型寫出一整個段落，頻頻使用 and、but、so 或非限定用法的 who、which、when、where、while 來連結句子（見規則 3）。

The third concert of the subscription series was given last evening, and a large audience was in attendance. Mr. Edward Appleton was the soloist, and the Boston Symphony Orchestra furnished the instrumental music. The former showed himself to be an artist of the first rank, while the latter proved itself fully deserving of its high reputation. The interest aroused by the series has been very gratifying to the Committee, and it is planned to give a similar series annually hereafter. The fourth concert will be given on Tuesday, May 10, when an equally attractive programme will be presented.

RULE 14 Avoid a succession of loose sentences:

This rule refers especially to loose sentences of a particular type, those consisting of two co-ordinate clauses, the second introduced by a conjunction or relative. Although single sentences of this type may be unexceptionable (see under Rule 4), a series soon becomes monotonous and tedious.

An unskilful writer will sometimes construct a whole paragraph of sentences of this kind, using as connectives *and, but, so,* and less frequently, *who, which, when, where,* and *while,* these last in non-restrictive senses (see under Rule 3).

The third concert of the subscription series was given last evening, and a large audience was in attendance. Mr. Edward Appleton was the soloist, and the Boston Symphony Orchestra furnished the instrumental music. The former showed himself to be an artist of the first rank, while the latter proved itself fully deserving of its high reputation. The interest aroused by the series has been very gratifying to the Committee, and it is planned to give a similar series annually hereafter. The fourth concert will be given on Tuesday, May 10, when an equally attractive programme will be presented.

II

ELEMENTARY PRINCIPLES OF COMPOSITION

RULE 8

RULE 9

RULE 10

RULE 11

RULE 12

RULE 13

RULE 14

RULE 15

預售系列的第三場演奏會昨晚揭幕，有大批觀眾出席。由愛德華・艾普頓先生擔任獨唱歌手，波士頓交響樂團以配樂妝點之。前者展現出自己在歌唱藝術方面一流的實力，而後者的表現證明自己名實相副。這系列演出引發大眾極高的興趣，評估委員會對此相當滿意，決定往後每年舉辦一次類似的系列活動。第四場演奏會將於五月十日星期二舉辦，為觀眾帶來同樣精采的表演。

（編註：較好的寫法請參考右頁。）

這個段落不僅讀來索然無味，架構也乏善可陳，不斷重複同樣的句構及陳述方式。同學可以拿規則 9 中引用段落的句子相比較，或參見其他散文名篇，如《浮華世界》中的「序」（題為「簾幕之前」，英文原文請見 page.111）。

如果同學寫作時發現段落中有許多上述類型的句構，應該盡量改寫成其他句構，例如：簡單句、由分號連接的兩個子句、包含兩個子句的完整句子，或包含三個子句的句子，以最精確、簡潔的方式呈現子句之間的關係。

以下是例文的修改示範：Attended by a large audience, the third concert of the subscription series was given last evening. Mr. Edward Appleton was the soloist with the Boston Symphony Orchestra furnishing the instrumental music. Mr. Appleton showed himself to be an artist of the first rank. Meanwhile, the Boston Symphony Orchestra proved itself fully deserving of its high reputation. Gratified by the interest aroused, the Committee has planned to give a similar series annually from now on. Tuesday, May 10 is when the fourth concert takes place with an equally attractive program.

RULE
8

RULE
9

RULE
10

RULE
11

RULE
12

RULE
13

RULE
14

RULE
15

Apart from its triteness and emptiness, the paragraph above is weak because of the structure of its sentences, with their mechanical symmetry and sing-song. Contrast with them the sentences in the paragraphs quoted under Rule 9, or in any piece of good English prose, as the preface (Before the Curtain) to *Vanity Fair*.

If the writer finds that he has written a series of sentences of the type described, he should recast enough of them to remove the monotony, replacing them by simple sentences, by sentences of two clauses joined by a semicolon, by periodic sentences of two clauses, by sentences, loose or periodic, of three clauses—whichever best represent the real relations of the thought.

《浮華世界・簾幕之前》

領班坐在戲台上的簾子前，對著底下鬧烘烘的市場，瞧了半晌，一陣深沉的悲哀冷不防地襲來。市場上有人吃喝、有人得了新歡就丟了舊愛，有人笑、有人哭。抽菸的、打架的、跳舞的、拉提琴的、欺詐人的，比比皆是。

有些是到處橫行的強梁漢子；有些是對女人拋媚眼的花花公子，也有扒手和到處巡邏的警察，還有走遍江湖吃遍十方的，在自己的攤子前面嚷嚷（這些全都是我的同行，真該死！）。鄉巴佬們抬頭緊盯穿著豔麗的舞者和可憐的翻筋斗老頭，而後面隨時都有三隻手的傢伙在掏他們口袋。

是啊，這就是浮華世界，在這鐵定沒什麼道德可言，更算不上是個快活之處，可以確定的是喧鬧無比。瞧瞧那些舞者和丑角下工後的表情，那個把臉上油漆洗淨才能坐下來和妻子吃飯的傻子，還有躲在簾幕後面那位小丑！幕起那霎，他便會倒栽蔥地問候：「你今天好嗎？」

Vanity Fair (Before The Curtain)

As the manager of the Performance sits before the curtain on the boards and looks into the Fair, a feeling of profound melancholy comes over him in his survey of the bustling place. There is a great quantity of eating and drinking, making love and jilting, laughing and the contrary, smoking, cheating, fighting, dancing and fiddling; there are bullies pushing about, bucks ogling the women, knaves picking pockets, policemen on the look-out, quacks (OTHER quacks, plague take them!) bawling in front of their booths, and yokels looking up at the tinselled dancers and poor old rouged tumblers, while the light-fingered folk are operating upon their pockets behind. Yes, this is VANITY FAIR; not a moral place certainly; nor a merry one, though very noisy. Look at the faces of the actors and buffoons when they come off from their business; and Tom Fool washing the paint off his cheeks before he sits down to dinner with his wife and the little Jack Puddings behind the canvas. The curtain will be up presently, and he will be turning over head and heels, and crying, "How are you?"

RULE
8

RULE
9

RULE
10

RULE
11

RULE
12

RULE
13

RULE
14

RULE
15

規則15 以類似結構陳述對等的概念。

本原則即所謂的「平行結構」，指在表達性質相似的內容或目的時，須使用類似的句構。因類似的句構能使讀者更易察覺內容和目的的相似性。《聖經》中有許多著名的例子❷，包含「十誡」、「天國八福」，以及〈主禱文〉中向上帝的祈禱。

不熟練的寫作者經常違反此原則，因為他／她以為英文寫作必須隨時變換表達方式。這點在重複敘述同一件事，做強調之用時並沒有錯，同學可以參閱規則10 中引用的段落。但除此之外，我們在寫作時應遵守「平行結構」的原則。

（✗）Formerly, science was taught by the text-book method, while now the laboratory method is employed.

（○）Formerly, science was taught by the text-book method; now it is taught by the laboratory method.

先前科學教育大都透過教科書進行，現在則以實驗為主。

學習小提醒 2

比如：Your kingdom come, Your will be done, on earth as it is in heaven. And for-give us our debts, as we also have forgiven our debtors.（願你的國降臨；願你的旨意行在地上，如同行在天上。免我們的債，如同我們免了人的債。）

RULE 15 Express co-ordinate ideas in similar form.

This principle, that of parallel construction, requires that expressions of similar content and function should be outwardly similar. The likeness of form enables the reader to recognize more readily the likeness of content and function. Familiar instances from the Bible are the Ten Commandments, the Beatitudes, and the petitions of the Lord's Prayer.

The unskillful writer often violates this principle, from a mistaken belief that he should constantly vary the form of his expressions. It is true that in repeating a statement in order to emphasize it he may have need to vary its form. For illustration, see the paragraph from Stevenson quoted under Rule 9. But apart from this, he should follow the principle of parallel construction.

(✕) Formerly, science was taught by the textbook method, while now the laboratory method is employed.

(◯) Formerly, science was taught by the textbook method; now it is taught by the laboratory method.

II

ELEMENTARY PRINCIPLES OF COMPOSITION

RULE 8
RULE 9
RULE 10
RULE 11
RULE 12
RULE 13
RULE 14
RULE 15

第一例句給人猶豫不決的感覺，作者似乎無法打定主意選用某種表達方式。第二個例句顯示作者至少做出了選擇並沿用之。

在這個原則之下，適用於所有並列字詞的冠詞或介系詞必須 (1) 只用於第一個詞之前，或 (2) 在每個詞語之前重複使用，以下皆是正確的用法：

（×）The French, the Italians, Spanish, and Portuguese
（○）The French, the Italians, the Spanish, and the Portuguese
法國人、義大利人、西班牙人和葡萄牙人

（×）In spring, summer, or in winter
（○）In spring, summer, or winter
（○）In spring, in summer, or in winter
在春天、夏天或冬天

both…and…、not…but…、not only…but also、either…or…、first,… second,… third,…、…and the like 等關聯詞語也應遵循同樣的文法結構，例如 both Henry and I、not silk, but a cheap substitute。下頁的前三個例子因為語序錯誤而違反此原則，最後一個例子則是前後使用了不同的句構。

The left-hand version gives the impression that the writer is undecided; he seems unable or afraid to choose one form of expression and hold to it. The right-hand version shows that the writer has at least made his choice and abided by it.

By this principle, an article or a preposition applying to all the members of a series must either be used only before the first term or else be repeated before each term.

(×) The French, the Italians, Spanish, and Portuguese
(○) The French, the Italians, the Spanish, and the Portuguese

(×) In spring, summer, or in winter
(○) In spring, summer, or winter
(○) In spring, in summer, or in winter

Correlative expressions (*both, and; not, but; not only, but also; either, or; first, second, third;* and the like) should be followed by the same grammatical construction, that is, virtually, by the same part of speech. (Such combinations as "both Henry and I, " "not silk, but a cheap substitute, " are obviously within the rule.) Many violations of this rule (as the first three below) arise from faulty arrangement; others (as the last) from the use of unlike constructions.

RULE
8

RULE
9

RULE
10

RULE
11

RULE
12

RULE
13

RULE
14

RULE
15

（×）It was both a long ceremony and very tedious.

（○）The ceremony was both long and tedious.
典禮冗長而無趣。

（×）A time not for words, but action.

（○）A time not for words, but for action.
此際勿坐而言，宜起而行。

（×）Either you must grant his request or incur his ill will.

（○）You must either grant his request or incur his ill will.
你要麼就答應他，要麼就承受他的怨念。

（×）My objections are, first, the injustice of the measure; second, that it is unconstitutional.

（○）My objections are, first, that the measure is unjust; second, that it is unconstitutional.
我反對的理由在於，其一，這個做法有失公允；其二，它與憲法相牴觸。

(×) It was both a long ceremony and very tedious.

(○) The ceremony was both long and tedious.

(×) A time not for words, but action.

(○) A time not for words, but for action.

(×) Either you must grant his request or incur his ill will.

(○) You must either grant his request or incur his ill will.

(×) My objections are, first, the injustice of the measure; second, that it is unconstitutional.

(○) My objections are, first, that the measure is unjust; second, that it is unconstitutional.

II

ELEMENTARY PRINCIPLES
OF COMPOSITION

RULE
8

RULE
9

RULE
10

RULE
11

RULE
12

RULE
13

RULE
14

RULE
15

同學也可參照規則 12 中的第三個例子，以及規則 13 中的最後一個例子。

那寫作若須陳述為數眾多的相似概念（比如有 20 個時），又該怎麼做呢？要連寫 20 個結構類似的句子嗎？若仔細想一想，同學可能會發現這是個假議題，因為 20 個概念定能分成好幾類，這樣一來只須把「平行結構」的原則套用到每個類別即可。除此之外，用表格呈現為數眾多的概念，也不失為一個好方法。

See also the third example under Rule 12 and the last under Rule 13.

It may be asked, what if a writer needs to express a very large number of similar ideas, say twenty? Must he write twenty consecutive sentences of the same pattern? On closer examination he will probably find that the difficulty is imaginary, that his twenty ideas can be classified in groups, and that he need apply the principle only within each group. Otherwise he had best avoid difficulty by putting his statements in the form of a table.

RULE
8

RULE
9

RULE
10

RULE
11

RULE
12

RULE
13

RULE
14

RULE
15

規則 16 把相關字詞放在一起。

字詞在句中的位置能夠表達字與字之間的關係。因此同學在寫作時應該盡量把相關的字詞放在一起，並將較不相關的字詞隔開。此外，句子的主詞和主要動詞之間，不應加入過長的片語或子句，若能將其移到句首則須為之。

（×）Wordsworth, in the fifth book of *The Excursion*, gives a minute description of this church.
（○）In the fifth book of *The Excursion*, Wordsworth gives a minute description of this church.
渥茲華斯在他長詩《漫遊》的第五部中把這棟教堂描繪得鉅細靡遺。

（×）Cast iron, when treated in a Bessemer converter, is changed into steel.
（○）By treatment in a Bessemer converter, cast iron is changed into steel.
鑄鐵經由貝塞麥轉爐法處理後，便煉成了鋼。

RULE 16 Keep related words together.

The position of the words in a sentence is the principal means of showing their relationship. The writer must therefore, so far as possible, bring together the words, and groups of words, that are related in thought, and keep apart those which are not so related. The subject of a sentence and the principal verb should not, as a rule, be separated by a phrase or clause that can be transferred to the beginning.

(✕) Wordsworth, in the fifth book of *The Excursion*, gives a minute description of this church.

(◯) In the fifth book of *The Excursion*, Wordsworth gives a minute description of this church.

(✕) Cast iron, when treated in a Bessemer converter, is changed into steel.

(◯) By treatment in a Bessemer converter, cast iron is changed into steel.

在上述兩個例子中，主詞和主要動詞之間插入的子句或片語破壞了句子的自然語序。不過，兩者之間加入的如果是關係子句或同位語，並不會違反這項原則。刻意中斷句子來吊讀者胃口的掉尾句 (periodic sentence) ❸亦不受此原則的限制。

原則上，關係代名詞必須緊跟在先行詞後：

（×）There was a look in his eye that boded mischief.
（○）In his eye was a look that boded mischief.
他露出使壞的眼神。

（×）He wrote three articles about his adventures in Spain, which were published in *Harper's Magazine*.
（○）He published in *Harper's Magazine* three articles about his adventures in Spain.
他在《哈潑雜誌》發表了三篇文章，分享他在西班牙的冒險經歷。

學習小提醒 3

英文中的掉尾句 (periodic sentence) 是一種比較正式的書面句型。其特點是將句子的次要成分提前，主要成分置後，形成整句的高潮，以取得設置懸念，吸引讀者非一口氣讀完不可的效果。例如《傲慢與偏見》的開場句：It is universally acknowledged that a single man in possession of a good fortune must be in want of a wife.（凡是有錢的單身漢，總想娶位太太，這是一條公認的真理。）

The objection is that the interposed phrase or clause needlessly interrupts the natural order of the main clause. Usually, however, this objection does not hold when the order is interrupted only by a relative clause or by an expression in apposition. Nor does it hold in periodic sentences in which the interruption is a deliberately used means of creating suspense (see examples under Rule 18).

The relative pronoun should come, as a rule, immediately after its antecedent.

(✕) There was a look in his eye that boded mischief.

(◯) In his eye was a look that boded mischief.

(✕) He wrote three articles about his adventures in Spain, which were published in *Harper's Magazine*.

(◯) He published in *Harper's Magazine* three articles about his adventures in Spain.

（×）This is a portrait of Benjamin Harrison, grandson of William Henry Harrison, who became President in 1889.

（○）This is a portrait of Benjamin Harrison, grandson of William Henry Harrison. He became President in 1889.

這是威廉・亨利・哈里遜的孫子——班傑明・哈里遜的肖像，他在 1889 年成為了總統。

若先行詞由好幾個詞組成，關係代名詞應緊接在這些詞之後，若語意不清則須設法釐清。例如：

（×）The grandson of William Henry Harrison, who

（○）William Henry Harrison's grandson, who

威廉・亨利・哈里遜的孫子，他……❹

（×）A proposal to amend the Sherman Act, which has been variously judged.

（○）A proposal, which has been variously judged, to amend the Sherman Act.

學習小提醒 4

在第一個例句中，who 的修飾對象不知道是 grandson 還是 William Henry Harrison，語意不清，因此需要改成第二種寫法來明確指出對象是誰。

> (✕) This is a portrait of Benjamin Harrison, grand-
> son of William Henry Harrison, who became President
> in 1889.
> (○) This is a portrait of Benjamin Harrison, grand-
> son of William Henry Harrison. He became President
> in 1889.

If the antecedent consists of a group of words, the relative comes at the end of the group, unless this would cause ambiguity.

> (✕) The grandson of William Henry Harrison, who
> (○) William Henry Harrison's grandson, who

> (✕) A proposal to amend the Sherman Act, which
> has been variously judged.
> (○) A proposal, which has been variously judged,
> to amend the Sherman Act.

RULE
16

RULE
17

RULE
18

（○）A proposal to amend the much-debated Sherman Act.
一項修訂《謝爾曼法案》的提案，目前毀譽參半。❺

名詞的同位語可置於先行詞和關係代名詞之間，因這種寫法不會導致語意不清。

The Duke of York, his brother, who was regarded with hostility by the Whigs
他的弟弟，即約克公爵，受到輝格黨的仇視。

修飾語應盡量靠近被修飾語，若數個修飾語同時修飾一個詞，也應遵照此原則安排語序，以釐清修飾關係，例如：

（×）All the members were not present.
（○）Not all the members were present.
並非全員出席。

學習小提醒 5

在第一個例句中，which has been variously judged 的修飾對象不知是 proposal（提案）還是 the Sherman Act（《謝爾曼法案》），令人難以理解，因此須改成後面兩個寫法來釐清語意。

（○）A proposal to amend the much-debated Sherman Act.

A noun in apposition may come between antecedent and relative, because in such a combination no real ambiguity can arise.

The Duke of York, his brother, who was regarded with hostility by the Whigs

Modifiers should come, if possible, next to the word they modify. If several expressions modify the same word, they should be so arranged that no wrong relation is suggested.

（×）All the members were not present.
（○）Not all the members were present.

RULE
16

RULE
17

RULE
18

（×）He only found two mistakes.

（○）He found only two mistakes.

他只找到兩處錯誤。

（×）Major R. E. Joyce will give a lecture on Tuesday evening in Bailey Hall, to which the public is invited, on "My Experiences in Mesopotamia" at eight P. M.

（○）On Tuesday evening at eight P. M., Major R. E. Joyce will give in Bailey Hall a lecture on "My Experiences in Mesopotamia." The public is invited.

喬伊斯少校將於週二晚上八點於貝禮廳演講〈美索不達米亞經驗談〉，歡迎大眾踴躍參加。

(✗) He only found two mistakes.

(○) He found only two mistakes.

(✗) Major R. E. Joyce will give a lecture on Tuesday evening in Bailey Hall, to which the public is invited, on "My Experiences in Mesopotamia" at eight P. M.

(○) On Tuesday evening at eight P. M., Major R. E. Joyce will give in Bailey Hall a lecture on "My Experiences in Mesopotamia." The public is invited.

RULE

16

RULE

17

RULE

18

規則 17 作摘要時要使用同一時態。

對戲劇情節作摘要時，一律使用現在式。對詩歌、故事或小說作摘要時，建議使用現在式，不過也可依個人喜好使用過去式。若以現在式作摘要，應用現在完成式描述先前發生的情節；若以過去式作摘要，則應使用過去完成式描述先前發生的情節。

An unforeseen chance prevents Friar John from delivering Friar Lawrence's letter to Romeo. Meanwhile, owing to her father's arbitrary change of the day set for her wedding, Juliet has been compelled to drink the potion on Tuesday night, with the result that Balthasar informs Romeo of her supposed death before Friar Lawrence learns of the non-delivery of the letter.

一樁始料未及的意外發生了，約翰修士沒能將勞倫斯修士的信交予羅密歐。同時茱麗葉則因父親強行更改婚期，被迫在週二晚上喝下了詐死毒藥。結果羅密歐在鮑爾德薩的告知下，誤信茱麗葉已死。勞倫斯修士後來才發現，給羅密歐的信件沒有送到。

RULE 17 In summaries, keep to one tense.

In summarizing the action of a drama, the writer should always use the present tense. In summarizing a poem, story, or novel, he should preferably use the present, though he may use the past if he prefers. If the summary is in the present tense, antecedent action should be expressed by the perfect; if in the past, by the past perfect.

An unforeseen chance prevents Friar John from delivering Friar Lawrence's letter to Romeo. Meanwhile, owing to her father's arbitrary change of the day set for her wedding, Juliet has been compelled to drink the potion on Tuesday night, with the result that Balthasar informs Romeo of her supposed death before Friar Lawrence learns of the non-delivery of the letter.

無論以何種時態作摘要，間接敘述或間接問句中的過去時態維持不變，如下：

The Friar confesses that it was he who married them. 修士坦承羅密歐和茱麗葉的證婚人正是自己。

除了這個例外，寫作摘要時皆須維持一致的時態。任意切換時態會給人拿不定主意的感覺（試比較規則15）。

在轉述他人的言詞時（如替文章或演講作摘要），應避免使用 he said（他說）、he stated（他表示）、the speaker added（講者還說）、the speaker then went to say（講者接下來說）、the author also thinks（作者也認為）等詞語。同學應於開頭就讓讀者知道你在作摘要，而不必用多餘的字詞重申此點。

在筆記、報紙、文學手冊中，摘要是不可或缺的一部分，而對小學生而言，用自己的話重述一個故事是很棒的練習。但在撰寫批判性文章或文學分析時，寫作者須注意不要整篇文章都在作摘要。用一兩個句子點明探討的主題或引用一些細節為例證當然無傷大雅，但寫作的目標應放在**「有組織地探討議題，並提出證**

But whichever tense be used in the summary, a past tense in indirect discourse or in indirect question remains unchanged.

> The Friar confesses that it was he who married them.

Apart from the exceptions noted, whichever tense the writer chooses, he should use throughout. Shifting from one tense to the other gives the appearance of uncertainty and irresolution (compare Rule 15).

In presenting the statements or the thought of some one else, as in summarizing an essay or reporting a speech, the writer should avoid intercalating such expressions as "he said," "he stated," "the speaker added," "the speaker then went on to say," "the author also thinks," or the like. He should indicate clearly at the outset, once for all, that what follows is summary, and then waste no words in repeating the notification.

In notebooks, in newspapers, in handbooks of literature, summaries of one kind or another may be indispensable, and for children in primary schools it is a useful exercise to retell a story in their own words. But in the criticism or interpretation of literature the writer should be careful to avoid dropping into summary. He may find it necessary to devote one or two sentences to indicating the subject, or the opening situation, of

據」，而非寫成一篇摘要為主，評論為輔的文章。

如果一次要探討數個文學作品，寫作時應避免逐一提及並評論每個文本，而應以寫作出具整體性的結論為目標。

the work he is discussing; he may cite numerous details to illustrate its qualities. But he should aim to write an orderly discussion supported by evidence, not a summary with occasional comment.

Similarly, if the scope of his discussion includes a number of works, he will as a rule do better not to take them up singly in chronological order, but to aim from the beginning at establishing general conclusions.

RULE
16

RULE
17

RULE
18

規則 18 將欲強調的字詞置於句尾。

當作者想強調句子中的詞語時，最好的方式便是將它放在句尾。

強調字詞未置於句尾	強調字詞置於句尾
Humanity has hardly advanced in fortitude since that time, though it has advanced in many other ways.	Humanity, since that time, has advanced in many other ways, but it has hardly advanced in fortitude.
自彼時起，人類在許多方面都有長足的進步，唯獨堅忍不拔的精神停滯不前。	

This steel is principally used for making razors, because of its hardness.	Because of its hardness, this steel is principally used in making razors.
這種鋼以堅硬著稱，因此常用來製作剃刀。	

置於強調位置的字詞通常是邏輯上的謂語 (logical predicate)，亦即句中的新資訊，如第二個例子所示。

RULE 18 Place the emphatic words of a sentence at the end.

The proper place in the sentence for the word, or group of words, which the writer desires to make most prominent is usually the end.

Humanity has hardly advanced in fortitude since that time, though it has advanced in many other ways.	Humanity, since that time, has advanced in many other ways, but it has hardly advanced in fortitude.

This steel is principally used for making razors, because of its hardness.	Because of its hardness, this steel is principally used in making razors.

The word or group of words entitled to this position of prominence is usually the logical predicate, that is, the new element in the sentence, as it is in the second example.

掉尾句的功能在於凸顯主要句子的內容，使整個句子
讀起來效果更佳，如下：

第二章

英文寫作的11個基本原則

規則
16

規則
17

規則
18

Four centuries ago, Christopher Columbus, one
of the Italian mariners whom the decline of their
own republics had put at the service of the world
and of adventure, seeking for Spain a westward
passage to the Indies as a set-off against the
achievements of Portuguese discoverers, lighted
on America.

四百年來，許多共和政體因國力衰退而派遣航海家到世界
各地探險，義大利籍的哥倫布便是其中之一。他替西班牙
尋找通往東印度群島的西向航道，意圖超越葡萄牙探險家
的功績，最後發現了美洲。

With these hopes and in this belief I would urge
you, laying aside all hindrance, thrusting away all
private aims, to devote yourself unswervingly
and unflinchingly to the vigorous and successful
prosecution of this war.

憑著這些希望和信念，我要勉勵諸位，排除萬難及一己之
私，堅定不移地投入這場必贏不可的聖戰。

The effectiveness of the periodic sentence arises from the prominence which it gives to the main statement.

Four centuries ago, Christopher Columbus, one of the Italian mariners whom the decline of their own republics had put at the service of the world and of adventure, seeking for Spain a westward passage to the Indies as a set-off against the achievements of Portuguese discoverers, lighted on America.

With these hopes and in this belief I would urge you, laying aside all hindrance, thrusting away all private aims, to devote yourself unswervingly and unflinchingly to the vigorous and successful prosecution of this war.

另一個強調詞語的方式則是置於句首。句中除主詞之外的任何成分置於句首時，都能達到強調的效果，例如：

Deceit or treachery he could never forgive.
他絕不能原諒欺騙或背叛他的人。

So vast and rude, fretted by the action of nearly three thousand years, the fragments of this architecture may often seem, at first sight, like works of nature.
這棟建築的殘跡在經歷近三千年的風霜歲月後仍開闊而粗獷，一眼望去就像大自然的傑作。

置於句首的主詞可能具有強調效果，但通常句中還會有其他強調成分。例如：

Great kings worshipped at his shrine,
偉大的國王都曾到他的聖祠朝拜

在這句中，kings 一字為重點的原因在於其字義及上下文，而非其在句中的位置。

The other prominent position in the sentence is the beginning. Any element in the sentence, other than the subject, may become emphatic when placed first.

> Deceit or treachery he could never forgive.

> So vast and rude, fretted by the action of nearly three thousand years, the fragments of this architecture may often seem, at first sight, like works of nature.

A subject coming first in its sentence may be emphatic, but hardly by its position alone. In the sentence,

> Great kings worshipped at his shrine,

the emphasis upon *kings* arises largely from its meaning and from the context.

將主詞置於述語 (predicate) **❻**的位置可達到刻意強調
的效果，如：

> Through the middle of the valley <u>flowed a wind-
> ing stream</u>. 山谷中央有條彎曲的河流流過。

「最重要的放最後」的原則不僅適用於句子中的字
詞，也適用於段落中的句子，以及一篇文章中的段
落。

述語指的是「一個句子中包含動詞以及為主詞提供資訊的部分」。

To receive special emphasis, the subject of a sentence must take the position of the predicate.

Through the middle of the valley flowed a winding stream.

The principle that the proper place for what is to be made most prominent is the end applies equally to the words of a sentence, to the sentences of a paragraph, and to the paragraphs of a composition.

RULE
16

RULE
17

RULE
18

想寫出滿級分的英文文章，你得學會——

- 段落寫作的黃金三結構：

  1. 主題句 (topic sentence)：首句就揭露段落主旨；

  2. 本文：解釋、發展主題句的概念；

  3. 末句：重新強調主題句，提出有力的結論。

- 使用精確而非抽象的字詞，才能啟動讀者的想像力！

- the fact that 不管出現在哪裡都是贅字，必須改寫！

- 多用肯定敘述、主動語態，除非必要才使用否定敘述、被動語態。

- 善用進階寫作技巧—「平行結構」來陳述對等的概念！

- 把相關字詞放一起，避免語意不清的窘狀！

第三章

寫作格式的
7 大注意事項

III

A FEW MATTERS OF FORM

寫作者在引述文獻、
用括號來補充主文內容，
以及引用別人所說的話時，
應該遵守本章要求的正確書寫格式。

注意事項 **1** 標題

標題下方要空一行，或留下等同於一行的空白。若使用橫格紙，換頁後要從第一行接著書寫。

注意事項 **2** 數字

日期或編號不必以英文拼寫，用阿拉伯數字或羅馬數字表示即可。

> 例如：
> August 9, 1918 (9 August 1918)
> 一九一八年八月九日
> Rule 3　規則三
> Chapter XII　第十二章
> 352nd Infantry　步兵三五二師

注意事項 **3** 括號

句子中若有括號夾注的詞語或句子，其標點方式與沒有插入括號時相同。括號內的句子應視為獨立句來標點，但句末的句號要省略，問號或驚嘆號則保留。

Headings.

Leave a blank line, or its equivalent in space, after the title or heading of a manuscript. On succeeding pages, if using ruled paper, begin on the first line.

 Numerals.

Do not spell out dates or other serial numbers. Write them in figures or in Roman notation, as may be appropriate.

August 9, 1918 (9 August 1918)
Rule 3
Chapter XII
352nd Infantry

 Parentheses.

A sentence containing an expression in parenthesis is punctuated, outside of the marks of parenthesis, exactly as if the expression in parenthesis were absent. The expression within is punctuated as if it stood by itself, except that the final stop is omitted unless it is a question mark or an exclamation point.

I went to his house yesterday (my third attempt to see him), but he had left town. 我昨天去了他家（這是我第三次去找他），但他出城去了。

He declares (and why should we doubt his good faith?) that he is now certain of success. 他宣稱（我們何須質疑他十足的信心？）自己一定會成功。

若括號內是獨立的完整句子，句號則須置於右括號之前。❶

注意事項 4 引文

直接引文來佐證論述時，引文須置於冒號之後，並於前後加上引號。

The provision of the Constitution is: "No tax or duty shall be laid on articles exported from any state."
此憲法條文指出：「由各州輸出的貨品不必課稅。」

學習小提醒 1

例如：This is my third failed attempt to visit him. (He's still out of town.) 這是我第三次去拜訪他，又撲空了。（他還沒回到鎮上）

> I went to his house yesterday (my third attempt to see him), but he had left town.
>
> He declares (and why should we doubt his good faith?) that he is now certain of success.

(When a wholly detached expression or sentence is parenthesized, the final stop comes before the last mark of parenthesis.)

4 Quotations.

Formal quotations, cited as documentary evidence, are introduced by a colon and enclosed in quotation marks.

> The provision of the Constitution is: "No tax or duty shall be laid on articles exported from any state."

引文若為同位語或動詞的直接受詞，前面應加逗號，
左右再加上引號。

I recall the maxim of La Rochefoucauld, "Grati-
tude is a lively sense of benefits to come."
我想起法國作家拉羅西弗可的銘言：「感恩是一切獲益的
活水源頭。」
Aristotle says, "Art is an imitation of nature."
亞里斯多德說：「藝術是對自然的模仿。」

引用整行或多行詩句時，要另起一行並將引文置中，
但無須加上引號。

Wordsworth's enthusiasm for the Revolution was
at first unbounded:
　　　　Bliss was it in that dawn to be alive,
　　　　But to be young was very heaven!
華茲華斯首先抒發對法國大革命的熱情：
　　　　能活在黎明時分是莫大福分
　　　　擁有青春年華更如置身天堂！

由 that 引導的引文為間接的陳述時（或稱「間接引
用」），無須引號，如下頁例句：

Quotations grammatically in apposition or the direct objects of verbs are preceded by a comma and enclosed in quotation marks.

> I recall the maxim of La Rochefoucauld, "Gratitude is a lively sense of benefits to come."
> Aristotle says, "Art is an imitation of nature."

Quotations of an entire line, or more, of verse, are begun on a fresh line and centered, but need not be enclosed in quotation marks.

> Wordsworth's enthusiasm for the Revolution was at first unbounded:
>
> > Bliss was it in that dawn to be alive,
> > But to be young was very heaven!

Quotations introduced by *that* are regarded as in indirect discourse and not enclosed in quotation marks.

Keats declares that beauty is truth, truth beauty.

濟慈認為美即是真，真即是美。

謬語和大眾熟知的文學典故無須引號。

These are the times that try men's souls. ❷

這些便是試煉人類靈魂的時刻。

He lives far from the madding crowd. ❸

他的居所遠離塵囂。

引用口語或俗語亦同。

注意事項 5 文獻出處

在須詳細註明出處的學術文章中，請先以縮寫表示常出現的文獻標題，再於文末以字母順序完整列出引用文獻。

學習小提醒 2

此句出自美國著名思想家湯瑪斯·潘恩（Thomas Paine）在美國獨立戰爭期間撰寫的愛國著作《北美的危機》（*The American Crisis*）。

學習小提醒 3

此句引用英國小說家哈代（Thomas Hardy）的長篇小說書名《遠離塵囂》（*Far from the Madding Crowd*）。

> Keats declares that beauty is truth, truth beauty.

Proverbial expressions and familiar phrases of literary origin require no quotation marks.

> These are the times that try men's souls.
> He lives far from the madding crowd.

The same is true of colloquialisms and slang.

5 References.

In scholarly work requiring exact references, abbreviate titles that occur frequently, giving the full forms in an alphabetical list at the end.

文獻出處通常置於括號或註腳，而非直接寫於句中。
除非特別指定，否則可將 act（幕）、scene（景）、line
（行）、book（冊）、volume（卷）、page（頁）等字刪去，
標點方式則舉例如下：

In the second scene of the third act 第三幕第二景
In III.ii（更好的寫法是將 III.ii 置於括號內，並置於句中
適當的位置）

After the killing of Polonius, Hamlet is placed under guard (IV.ii. 14). 哈姆雷特在殺死波隆尼爾後便受
到監視。（第四幕第二景第 14 行）

2 Samuel i:17-27 《撒母耳記下》第一章 17-27 節

Othello II.iii. 264-267, III.iii. 155-161. 《奧賽羅》第
二幕第三景 264-267 行、第三幕第三景 155-161 行。

注意
事項 **6** **單字跨行的斷字原則**

若在一行的結尾有空間容納單字的一個或多個音節，

As a general practice, give the references in parenthesis or in footnotes, not in the body of the sentence. Omit the words *act*, *scene*, *line*, *book*, *volume*, *page*, except when referring by only one of them. Punctuate as indicated below.

In the second scene of the third act
In III.ii (still better, simply insert III.ii in parenthesis at the proper place in the sentence)

After the killing of Polonius, Hamlet is placed under guard (IV.ii. 14).

2 Samuel i:17–27

Othello II.iii. 264–267, III.iii. 155–161.

6 Syllabication.

If there is room at the end of a line for one or more syllables of a word, but not for the whole word, divide the word, unless this involves cutting off only a single letter, or cutting off only

但放不下整個字，可將其餘的音節置於下一行的開頭，關於此點沒有一條萬用的切字法則，但同學可參照以下幾種方式：

(a) 依照單字的組成切分：

know-ledge（不是 knowl-edge）、Shake-speare（不是 Shakes-peare）、de-scribe（不是 des-cribe）、atmo-sphere（不是 atmos-phere）

(b) 在母音後切分：

edi-ble（不是 ed-ible）、propo-sition、ordi-nary、espe-cial、reli-gious、oppo-nents、regu-lar、classi-fi-ca-tion（也可以切成三個部分）、deco-rative、presi-dent

(c) 在重複的字母之間切分：

Apen-nines、Cincin-nati、refer-ring
諸如 tell-ing 之類的構詞則例外

(d) 若 -ed 字尾中的 e 不發音，則不可在 ed 之前切分：

（○）treat-ed
（×）roam-ed、nam-ed

two letters of a long word. No hard and fast rule for all words can be laid down. The principles most frequently applicable are:

(a) Divide the word according to its formation: know-ledge (not knowl-edge); Shake-speare (not Shakes-peare); de-scribe (not des-cribe); atmo-sphere (not atmos-phere);

(b) Divide "on the vowel:" edi-ble (not ed-ible); propo-sition; ordi-nary; espe-cial; reli-gious; oppo-nents; regu-lar; classi-fi-ca-tion (three divisions allowable); deco-rative; presi-dent;

(c) Divide between double letters, unless they come at the end of the simple form of the word: Apen-nines; Cincin-nati; refer-ring; but tell-ing.

(d) Do not divide before final -ed if the e is silent: treat-ed (but not roam-ed or nam-ed).

若遇字音相連的狀況可參考下列例字：

for-tune、pic-ture、sin-gle、presump-tuous（放肆的）、illus-tration、sub-stan-tial、indus-try、instruc-tion、sug-ges-tion、incen-diary（煽動的）

只要閱讀幾頁印刷工整的英文書，同學就能了解音節切分的原則了。

注意事項 **7** 書名、詩名、戲劇名

文學作品的標題在學術文章中通常使用斜體字，並將首字母大寫。編輯和出版社則有各自習慣的用法，有些使用斜體字與首字母大寫，有些則用正體字與首字母大寫；有些會加引號，有些則不加。除非投稿的期刊另有規定，否則使用斜體字為宜（手寫時則畫底線）。列出書名時前面若有所有格，則須省略書名中的 A 或 The。

The Iliad、the Odyssey、As You Like It、To a Skylark、The Newcomes、A Tale of Two Cities、Dickens's Tale of Two Cities

（《伊利亞德》、《奧德賽》、《皆大歡喜》、《致雲雀》、《紐坎家族》、《雙城記》；狄更斯的《雙城記》）

The treatment of consonants in combination is best
shown from examples:
for-tune; pic-ture; sin-gle; presump-tuous;
illus-tration; sub-stan-tial (either division); indus-try;
instruc-tion; sug-ges-tion; incen-diary.

The student will do well to examine the syllable-division in a
number of pages of any carefully printed book.

Titles.

For the titles of literary works, scholarly usage prefers italics
with capitalized initials. The usage of editors and publishers
varies, some using italics with capitalized initials, others using
Roman with capitalized initials and with or without quotation
marks. Use italics (indicated in manuscript by underscoring),
except in writing for a periodical that follows a different practice. Omit initial *A* or *The* from titles when you place the possessive before them.

The Iliad; the Odyssey; As You Like It; To a Skylark;
The Newcomes; A Tale of Two Cities; Dickens's Tale of
Two Cities.

寫作正式的英語文章時，
你應該注意——

◎ 當括號內是獨立句時，句末句號要省略，問號
和驚嘆號則應該保留。

◎ 直接引文時，引文前面應該加上冒號，左右再
加上引號；間接引文時，則可省略左右引號。

◎ 文章中出現書名 詩名 劇名時 要使用斜體字。

第四章

經常誤用／濫用的
50 個字詞

IV

WORDS AND EXPRESSIONS
COMMONLY MISUSED

本章列出許多連母語人士都會誤用的字詞，
以及大家濫用成習的用語。
這類錯誤通常需要整句改寫，
請讀者詳細觀摩史壯克教授提供的修改範例。

本章列出的用語如 like I did（詳見第 188 頁）等等「菜英文」不該在文章中出現，而 case、factor、feature、interesting、one of the most 等詞語用對地方時則沒問題，但同學經常在不該使用之處誤用。寫作的目的在於清楚傳達個人的想法，因此不該為了省麻煩而套用某些公式。**寫作時若發現自己誤用了某個詞語，最好的方式不是找另一個字來替代，而是更換一種表達方式，或重寫整個句子**，一如規則 12、13 以及下列的例子。

易誤用字詞 1　All right（好的；去吧）

道地而常見的口語，表示「好的」（Agreed）或「去吧」（Go ahead）時可以使用，其他狀況則盡量不用，注意 all 和 right 必須分開。

易誤用字詞 2　As good or better than（一樣好，或者更好）

使用這類詞語時需調整語序，例如下頁例句：

Some of the forms here listed, as *like I did*, are downright bad English; others, as the split infinitive, have their defenders, but are in such general disfavor that it is at least inadvisable to use them; still others, as *case, factor, feature, interesting, one of the most*, are good in their place, but are constantly obtruding themselves into places where they have no right to be. If the writer will make it his purpose from the beginning to express accurately his own individual thought, and will refuse to be satisfied with a ready-made formula that saves him the trouble of doing so, this last set of expressions will cause him little trouble. But if he finds that in a moment of inadvertence he has used one of them, his proper course will probably be not to patch up the sentence by substituting one word or set of words for another, but to recast it completely, as illustrated in a number of examples below and in others under Rules 12 and 13.

All right.

Idiomatic in familiar speech as a detached phrase in the sense, "Agreed," or "Go ahead." In other uses better avoided. Always written as two words.

As good or better than.

Expressions of this type should be corrected by rearranging the sentence.

（×）My opinion is as good or better than his.

（○）My opinion is as good as his, or better.

（○）My opinion is as good as his, if not better.

我的意見就算沒比他的好，至少也一樣好。

易誤用字詞 3　As to whether（是否）

寫成 whether（是否）即可，參見規則 13。

易誤用字詞 4　Bid（告訴；吩咐）

後面若接不定詞須省略 to ❶，當作「告訴；吩咐」用時過去式為 bade。

易誤用字詞 5　But（但是）

過度將 but 作為連接詞使用違反了規則 14，因為以 but 構成的鬆散句必能改寫成以 although 構成的掉尾句，一如規則 4 所述。

學習小提醒 ❶

例如：He bade them leave at once. 他請他們馬上離開。

(×) My opinion is as good or better than his.

(○) My opinion is as good as his, or better.

(○) My opinion is as good as his, if not better.

WORDS AND EXPRESSIONS
COMMONLY MISUSED

3 As to whether.

Whether is sufficient; see under Rule 13.

4 Bid.

Takes the infinitive without *to*. The past tense in the sense, "ordered," is *bade*.

5 But.

The too frequent use of *but* as a conjunction leads to the fault discussed under Rule 14. A loose sentence formed with *but* can always be converted into a periodic sentence formed with *although*, as illustrated under Rule 4.

在一個句子中連用兩個 but 會使文句不通順，所以寫作者應該調動語序。

（✗）America had vast resources, but she seemed almost wholly unprepared for war. But within a year she had created an army of four million men.

（○）America seemed almost wholly unprepared for war, but she had vast resources. Within a year she had created an army of four million men.

美國起初看來完全沒為戰爭做好準備，但她擁有豐富的資源，在一年內培育了四百萬大軍。

易誤用
字詞 **6** **Case**（狀況；案例）

《牛津簡明辭典》對這個詞的定義為：instance of a thing's occurring; usual state of affairs（某事發生的場合；事件的普遍狀況）。依照這兩種定義來看，case 通常是冗詞。

（✗）In many cases, the rooms were poorly ventilated.

（○）Many of the rooms were poorly ventilated.

許多房間通風奇差。

Particularly awkward is the following of one *but* by another, making a contrast to a contrast or a reservation to a reservation. This is easily corrected by re-arrangement.

(×) America had vast resources, but she seemed almost wholly unprepared for war. But within a year she had created an army of four million men.

(○) America seemed almost wholly unprepared for war, but she had vast resources. Within a year she had created an army of four million men.

 Case.

The *Concise Oxford Dictionary* begins its definition of this word: "instance of a thing's occurring; usual state of affairs." In these two senses, the word is usually unnecessary.

(×) In many cases, the rooms were poorly ventilated.

(○) Many of the rooms were poorly ventilated.

（×）It has rarely been the case that any mistake has been made.

（○）Few mistakes have been made.

幾乎沒什麼失誤發生。

有興趣的同學可參閱 Wood, *Suggestions to Authors*，第 68-71 頁、Quiller-Couch, *The Art of Writing*，第 103-106 頁。

易誤用字詞 7 Certainly（當然；無疑地）

有些同學在寫作時濫用 very 或 certainly 來加強語氣。說話時濫用這類詞彙已是壞習慣，寫作時更應避免。

易誤用字詞 8 Character（性格）

這是用了只會大幅增加冗贅程度的冗詞贅字。

（×）Acts of a hostile character

不友善性格造成的行為

（○）Hostile acts　充滿敵意的行為

(×) It has rarely been the case that any mistake has been made.

(○) Few mistakes have been made.

See Wood, *Suggestions to Authors*, pp. 68–71, and Quiller-Couch, *The Art of Writing*, pp. 103–106.

Certainly.

Used indiscriminately by some writers, much as others use *very*, to intensify any and every statement. A mannerism of this kind, bad in speech, is even worse in writing.

8 Character.

Often simply redundant, used from a mere habit of wordiness.

(×) Acts of a hostile character

(○) Hostile acts

易誤用字詞 9 Claim（宣稱；要求；索取）

作為名詞受詞用時，意謂「提出對……的所有權」(lay claim to)，若要清楚傳達此意義，後面可接附屬子句，例如：He claimed that he was the sole surviving heir.（他宣稱自己是唯一在世的繼承人。）但這句話改用 claim to be 會更好，例如：He claimed to be the sole surviving heir. 此外，避免用 claim 來替代 declare、maintain 或 charge。

易誤用字詞 10 Clever（機靈的）

這個詞濫用的情況也很嚴重，建議只作「耍小聰明」使用。

易誤用字詞 11 Compare（比較；對比）

片語 compare to 用來指出兩個本質不同的事物的相似之處；compare with 則是比較兩個本質相同事物的不同之處。比如我們可以將人生比擬為 (compare to) 朝聖之旅 (pilgrimage)、戲劇 (drama) 或戰爭 (battle)；美國國會可以與英國國會相比較，找出相異之處 (be compared with)。此外，巴黎曾被比喻為古代的雅典 (be compared to)，也能與現代的倫敦互相比較 (be compared with)。

Claim.

With object-noun, means *lay claim to*. May be used with a dependent clause if this sense is clearly involved: "He claimed that he was the sole surviving heir." (But even here, "claimed to be" would be better.)

Not to be used as a substitute for *declare*, *maintain*, or *charge*.

 **Clever.**

This word has been greatly overused; it is best restricted to ingenuity displayed in small matters.

Compare.

To *compare to* is to point out or imply resemblances, between objects regarded as essentially of different order; to *compare with* is mainly to point out differences, between objects regarded as essentially of the same order. Thus life has been compared to a pilgrimage, to a drama, to a battle; Congress may be compared with the British Parliament. Paris has been compared to ancient Athens; it may be compared with modern London.

易誤用 字詞 12 **Consider**（考慮；認為）

作「認為」(believe to be) 用時，後面不加 as，例如：I consider him thoroughly competent.（我認為他必能勝任）。而在以下這句話中：The lecturer considered Cromwell first as soldier and second as administrator.（講者先想到克倫威爾是個軍人，才想到他是個指揮官），consider 則有 examine（審視）或 discuss（論述）之意。

易誤用 字詞 13 **Data**（資料）

Data 本身就是複數名詞，一如 phenomena（現象）和 strata（地層；階層）。

> These data were tabulated. 那些資料已列表呈現。

易誤用 字詞 14 **Dependable**（可靠的）

這個字沒有必要，宜用 reliable 或 trustworthy 取代。

 **Consider.**

Not followed by *as* when it means "believe to be." "I consider him thoroughly competent." Compare, "The lecturer considered Cromwell first as soldier and second as administrator," where "considered" means "examined" or "discussed."

 Data.

A plural, like *phenomena* and *strata*.

These data were tabulated.

14 Dependable.

A needless substitute for *reliable, trustworthy.*

易誤用字詞 **15** Divided into（分成…）

不宜與 composed of（由……組成）混用，例如：戲劇分成許多幕 (Plays are divided into acts.)，詩則由詩節組成 (Poems are composed of stanzas.)。

易誤用字詞 **16** Due to（歸功於）

常被誤用為副詞片語表示 through（透過）、because of❷（因為）或 owing to（起因於）之意，例如：

（×）He lost the first game, due to carelessness.
（○）He lost the first game because of carelessness.
他因為大意而輸掉了第一場比賽。

due to 應該用來修飾名詞，或當作述語，例如：This invention is due to Edison.（這項發明應歸功於愛迪生）或 losses due to preventable fires（可預防的火災造成的損失）。

學習小提醒 **2**

當主句子的動詞不是 be 動詞，而是普通的動詞時，應該使用 because of 和 owing to，反之則應該用 due to。例如：

（×）Connie cannot go to lunch due to her work.
（○）Connie cannot go to lunch because of her work.

15 Divided into.

Not to be misused for *composed of.* The line is sometimes difficult to draw; doubtless plays are divided into acts, but poems are composed of stanzas.

16 Due to.

Incorrectly used for *through, because of,* or *owing to*, in adverbial phrases:

(×) He lost the first game, due to carelessness.
(○) He lost the first game because of carelessness.

In correct use related as predicate or as modifier to a particular noun: "This invention is due to Edison;" "losses due to preventable fires."

易誤用字詞 **17** Effect（結果：引起某事發生）

當名詞用時，意近 result（結果）；作動詞用時則是
bring about（引起某事發生）或 accomplish（達成）之意（切
勿與 affect 混淆，affect 雖然也是動詞，但意思是「影響」❸）。
effect 作名詞用時也常被濫用於時尚、音樂、繪畫與
其他藝術相關的文章，例如 an Oriental effect（東方效
應）、effects in pale green（淡綠色的效果）、very delicate effects（非常精緻的效果）、broad effects（廣泛的效
應）、subtle effects（微妙的效果）、a charming effect
was produced by……（被……營造出迷人的效果），寫作者
如果有明確的意圖，就不會用以上模糊的論述閃躲。

易誤用字詞 **18** Etc.（如此等等）

與 and the rest（諸如此類）、and so forth（等等）同義，
若列舉的項目不夠多，不應加上此字來使語意模糊。
此外，若已完整列出所有項目，也不應使用 etc.，更
不可將其當作讓語氣完整的助詞，隨意置於句尾。

學習小提醒 **3**

effect 較少作動詞使用，通常出現在正式的文章中，表示「使某件事情
發生」，例如：The government will effect some new environmental policies
starting next year.（政府將從明年開始實施一些新的環境政策）affect 則是
表示「對某事的影響」，例如：The cancer affected every aspect of her life.（罹
患癌症影響了她生活的許多層面）

Effect.

As noun, means *result*; as verb, means to *bring about*, *accomplish* (not to be confused with *affect*, which means "to influence").

As noun, often loosely used in perfunctory writing about fashions, music, painting, and other arts: "an Oriental effect;" "effects in pale green;" "very delicate effects;" "broad effects;" "subtle effects;" "a charming effect was produced by." The writer who has a definite meaning to express will not take refuge in such vagueness.

18 Etc.

Equivalent to *and the rest*, *and so forth*, and hence not to be used if one of these would be insufficient, that is, if the reader would be left in doubt as to any important particulars. Least open to objection when it represents the last terms of a list already given in full, or immaterial words at the end of a quotation.

以 such as（譬如）、for example（舉例來說）或其他類似用語引導的項目後方不可使用 etc. ❹。

易誤用字詞 19 Fact（事實）

這個字只能用來指稱可直接證實的事件，不可用於主觀判斷。例如某個事件發生的日期、物體的熔點都是事實，但「拿破崙是當代最偉大的將領」、「加州的天氣很棒」，即使再多人認同，也不能稱作 fact。

關於 the fact that 的說明，請參見規則 13。

易誤用字詞 20 Factor（因素；要素）

常見的濫用字詞，包含 factor 的句子通常能以更直接或更道地的用法取代。

學習小提醒 4

由 such as 所代出的清單，後面不能使用 etc.，例如：

（×）The money is to cover costs such as transportation, shopping, accommodation, etc.

（○）The money is to cover costs such as transportation, shopping, and accommodation. 這筆錢是用來支付交通費、購物和住宿費。

At the end of a list introduced by *such as, for example*, or any similar expression, *etc.* is incorrect.

Fact.

Use this word only of matters of a kind capable of direct verification, not of matters of judgment. That a particular event happened on a given date, that lead melts at a certain temperature, are facts. But such conclusions as that Napoleon was the greatest of modern generals, or that the climate of California is delightful, however incontestable they may be, are not properly facts.

On the formula *the fact that*, see under Rule 13.

 Factor.

A hackneyed word; the expressions of which it forms part can usually be replaced by something more direct and idiomatic.

（×）His superior training was the great factor in his winning the match.

他受過的優良訓練，是贏得比賽最大的因素。

（○）He won the match by being better trained.

他接受的訓練較為優良，因此贏得了比賽。

（×）Heavy artillery has become an increasingly important factor in deciding battles.

重型火砲在重大戰役中已成為了一個益加重要的因素。

（○）Heavy artillery has played a constantly larger part in deciding battles.

重型火炮在重大戰役中扮演的角色日益吃重。

易誤用 字詞 21 Feature（特徵；特色）

一如 factor 是個濫用字，無法提供太多實質意義。

（×）A feature of the entertainment especially worthy of mention was the singing of Miss A.

這項表演值得一提的特色就是 A 小姐出場獻唱。

（同樣的字數倒不如描述 A 小姐唱了什麼歌，或如果表演已經結束，也可描述她獻唱的情形。）

(×) His superior training was the great factor in his winning the match.

(○) He won the match by being better trained.

(×) Heavy artillery has become an increasingly important factor in deciding battles.

(○) Heavy artillery has played a constantly larger part in deciding battles.

21 Feature.

Another hackneyed word; like *factor* it usually adds nothing to the sentence in which it occurs.

(×) A feature of the entertainment especially worthy of mention was the singing of Miss A.

(Better use the same number of words to tell what Miss A. sang, or if the programme has already been given, to tell how she sang.)

易誤用字詞 22 Fix（繫牢；固定）

美式口語中的常用來當作 arrange（安排）、prepare（準備）、mend（修理），但在寫作時只應使用其最直接的意義：fasten（繫牢）或、make firm（固定）或 im-movable（固定）❺。

易誤用字詞 23 He is a man who

典型的冗詞，參見規則 13。

（×）He is a man who is very ambitious.
他是一個很有抱負的人。
（○）He is very ambitious. 他很有抱負。

（×）Spain is a country which I have always wanted to visit. 西班牙是個我總是想要拜訪的國家。
（○）I have always wanted to visit Spain.
我一直想去西班牙看看。

學習小提醒 **5**

例如：「把鏡子固定在牆上」宜用 fix the bookcase to the wall，「修理裂開的水管」宜用 mend the burst pipe。

Fix.

Colloquial in America for *arrange*, *prepare*, *mend*. In writing restrict it to its literary senses, *fasten*, *make firm* or *immovable*, etc.

 He is a man who.

A common type of redundant expression; see Rule 13.

(×) He is a man who is very ambitious.

(○) He is very ambitious.

(×) Spain is a country which I have always wanted to visit.

(○) I have always wanted to visit Spain.

易誤用字詞 24 Interesting（有趣的）

避免這個敷衍的詞，與其跟別人說你要講的事很有趣，不如講得很有趣。

（×）An interesting story is told of
有個有趣的故事
（○）什麼都別說，直接講個有趣的故事

（×）In connection with the anticipated visit of Mr. B. to America, it is interesting to recall that he...
說到 B 先生造訪美國，我想到一件有趣的事，他⋯⋯
（○）Mr. B., who it is expected will soon visit America 很快就要造訪美國的 B 先生⋯⋯

易誤用字詞 25 Kind of

不可用來取代置於形容詞和動詞前的 rather ❻。除非

學習小提醒 ❻

kind of 在口語中很常用來作「稍微」解，但在正式的文章中應該盡量避免，最好用 rather 來取代，例如：

（×）We were kind of disappointed at the results.
（○）We were rather disappointed at the results. 我們對結果有些失望。

24 Interesting.

Avoid this word as a perfunctory means of introduction. Instead of announcing that what you are about to tell is interesting, make it so.

(✗) An interesting story is told of
(◯) (Tell the story without preamble.)

(✗) In connection with the anticipated visit of Mr. B. to America, it is interesting to recall that he
(◯) Mr. B., who it is expected will soon visit America

25 Kind of.

Not to be used as a substitute for *rather* (before adjectives and

文章較不正式，否則也不可用來取代名詞前的 some-thing like。建議只使用其字面義（一種……），例如：Amber is a kind of fossil resin.（琥珀是一種樹脂化石）或 I dislike that kind of notoriety.（我討厭那種惡名）。sort of（一種……）的用法與此相似。

易誤用字詞 26 Less（較少）

不該與 fewer 混淆。

（✕）He had less men than in the previous campaign.

（○）He had fewer men than in the previous campaign.

他的人手比上次競選活動還少。

Less 指的是「程度」，fewer 指的則是「數量」。His troubles are less than mine 意謂「他的問題沒我的嚴重」；His troubles are fewer than mine 指的則是「他的問題沒我這麼多」。不過 The signers of the petition were less than a hundred（簽署請願書的人數不足一百）則是正確的用法，因為 a hundred（一百）這樣的整數可視為集合名詞，而 less 在此可表示「程度」或「數量」較少。

verbs), or except in familiar style, for *something like* (before nouns). Restrict it to its literal sense: "Amber is a kind of fossil resin;" "I dislike that kind of notoriety." The same holds true of *sort of*.

26 Less.

Should not be misused for *fewer*.

(✕) He had less men than in the previous campaign
(◯) He had fewer men than in the previous campaign

Less refers to quantity, *fewer* to number. "His troubles are less than mine" means "His troubles are not so great as mine." "His troubles are fewer than mine" means "His troubles are not so numerous as mine." It is, however, correct to say, "The signers of the petition were less than a hundred," where the round number *a hundred* is something like a collective noun, and *less* is thought of as meaning a less quantity or amount.

易誤用字詞 27 Like（像）

要避免和 as 混淆。Like 後頭接的是名詞和代名詞；在片語及子句前表示相同意義的則是 as。

（×）We spent the evening like in the old days.
（○）We spent the evening as in the old days.
我們就像從前一樣度過夜晚的時光。

（×）He thought like I did.
（○）He thought as I did.
（○）He thought like me.
他的想法與我相同。

（×）As most people, I'd prefer to have enough money not to work.
（○）Like most people, I'd prefer to have enough money not to work.
（○）As most people would, I'd prefer to have enough money not to work.
和大多數人一樣，我喜歡擁有足夠的錢，可以不用工作。

27 Like.

Not to be misused for *as*. *Like* governs nouns and pronouns; before phrases and clauses the equivalent word is *as*.

(✗) We spent the evening like in the old days.
(○) We spent the evening as in the old days.

(✗) He thought like I did.
(○) He thought as I did.
(○) He thought like me.

(✗) As most people, I'd prefer to have enough money not to work.
(○) Like most people, I'd prefer to have enough money not to work.
(○) As most people would, I'd prefer to have enough money not to work.

易誤用字詞 28 Literal, literally（完全是；根本是）

常被誤用來誇大其詞或增強語氣。

> （×）A literal flood of abuse.
> （○）A flood of abuse. 一連串的責罵。

> （×）Literally dead with fatigue
> （○）Almost dead with fatigue
> （○）dead tired 快累死了。

易誤用字詞 29 Lose out（輸掉）

本意是比 lose 更強烈的說法，但因為太常用反而效果不佳，相同的例子包括 try out（嘗試）、win out（贏得）、sign up（報名參加）、register up（註冊）。另一些動詞加上 out 和 up 則成為意思與原來不同的習語，例如：

28 Literal, literally.

Often incorrectly used in support of exaggeration or violent metaphor.

(✗) A literal flood of abuse.
(○) A flood of abuse.

(✗) Literally dead with fatigue
(○) Almost dead with fatigue
(○) dead tired

29 Lose out.

Meant to be more emphatic than *lose*, but actually less so, because of its commonness. The same holds true of *try out*, *win out*, *sign up*, *register up*. With a number of verbs, out and up form idiomatic combinations:

find out 發現	find 找到
run out 耗盡	run 奔跑
turn out 結果……	turn 轉動
cheer up 振奮	cheer 歡呼
dry up 枯竭	dry 晾乾、烘乾
make up 組成、捏造、化妝……	make 製作

但 lose 和 lose out 的意思並沒有不同。

易誤用字詞 30 Nature（性格）

如 character 一般常是冗詞。

（×）Acts of a hostile nature
不友善性格造成的行為
（○）Hostile acts 充滿敵意的行為

許多文章中常出現 a lover of nature（愛好大自然的人）
和 poems about nature（描寫大自然的詩句）等意義含糊
的用語，除非後面有更具體的敘述，讀者會難以判斷
這些詩是和自然風景、鄉村生活、夕陽、無人的荒野，
還是和松鼠的習性有關。

find out	find
run out	run
turn out	turn
cheer up	cheer
dry up	dry
make up	make

each distinguishable in meaning from the simple verb. *Lose out* is not.

30 Nature.

Often simply redundant, used like *character*.

(✗) Acts of a hostile nature
(◯) Hostile acts

Often vaguely used in such expressions as a "lover of nature;" "poems about nature." Unless more specific statements follow, the reader cannot tell whether the poems have to do with natural scenery, rural life, the sunset, the untracked wilderness, or the habits of squirrels.

易誤用字詞31 **Near by**（在附近）

作副詞片語用，有些人認為這不是優美的英文，即使 close by 和 hard by（兩者皆指「附近」）的用法似乎能為其辯護。寫作時使用 near 或 near at hand 即可，有時甚至更好。

此外，Near by 不可當形容詞用，應使用 neighboring。

易誤用字詞32 **Oftentimes, ofttimes**（時常）

過時的用語，用 often 即可。

易誤用字詞33 **One hundred and one**（101）

注意這類數字中的 and 皆須保留，以符合英語長期以來的固定用法。

易誤用字詞34 **One of the most**（最⋯⋯的之一）

避免在文章或段落的開頭使用，例如 One of the most interesting developments of modern science is⋯（現代科學其中一項最有趣的發展是⋯⋯），或 Switzerland is one of

Near by.

Adverbial phrase, not yet fully accepted as good English, though the analogy of *close by* and *hard by* seems to justify it. *Near*, or *near at hand*, is as good, if not better.

Not to be used as an adjective; use *neighboring*.

32 Oftentimes, ofttimes.

Archaic forms, no longer in good use. The modern word is *often*.

33 One hundred and one.

Retain the *and* in this and similar expressions, in accordance with the unvarying usage of English prose from Old English times.

34 One of the most.

Avoid beginning essays or paragraphs with this formula, as, "One of the most interesting developments of modern science is, etc.;" "Switzerland is one of the most interesting countries the most interesting countries of Europe（瑞士是歐洲最有趣的國家之一）。這種寫法文法上並沒有錯，卻顯得陳腔濫調、不夠有力。

易誤用字詞 35 People（人民）

People 這個詞常帶政治意義，注意不要與 the public（大眾）混淆。「人民」(the people) 可以支持或反對政治，「大眾」(the public) 則可欣賞藝術或上街血拼。

易誤用字詞 36 Phase（階段；時期）

指的是「轉變或發展的階段」，例如 the phases of the moon（月相）、the last phase（最後階段），不可用來指 aspect（方面）或 topic（主題）。

（×）Another phase of the subject
主題的另一個階段
（○）Another point (another question)
另一個論點（議題）

of Europe." There is nothing wrong in this; it is simply thread-bare and forcible-feeble.

35 People.

The people is a political term, not to be confused with *the public*. From the people comes political support or opposition; from the public comes artistic appreciation or commercial patronage.

36 Phase.

Means a stage of transition or development: "the phases of the moon;" "the last phase." Not to be used for *aspect* or *topic*.

(×) Another phase of the subject
(○) Another point (another question)

易誤用字詞 37 **Possess**（擁有）

不要僅用來代替 have 或 own。

（×）He possessed great courage.
他擁有許多勇氣
（○）He had great courage (was very brave).
他很勇敢

（×）He was the fortunate possessor of
他是……幸運的擁有者
（○）He owned 他擁有

易誤用字詞 38 **Respective, respectively**（分別是……）

這兩個詞最好直接省略。

（×）Works of fiction are listed under the names of their respective authors.
（○）Works of fiction are listed under the names of their authors. 小說類的作品列於作者姓名底下。

37 Possess.

Not to be used as a mere substitute for *have* or *own*.

(×) He possessed great courage.
(O) He had great courage (was very brave).

(×) He was the fortunate possessor of
(O) He owned

38 Respective, respectively.

These words may usually be omitted with advantage.

(×) Works of fiction are listed under the names of their respective authors.
(O) Works of fiction are listed under the names of their authors.

（×）The one mile and two mile runs were won by Jones and Cummings respectively.

（○）The one mile and two mile runs were won by Jones and by Cummings. 瓊斯贏得了一英哩路跑的冠軍，兩英哩路跑的贏家則是康明斯。

在某些正式的寫作形式，如幾何學證明中，respectively 可能是必須使用的單字，但一般的寫作中通常無須使用。

易誤用字詞39 Should（應該；會）

參見第 212 頁 would。

易誤用字詞40 So（多麼）

寫作時勿濫用 so 來加強語氣，例如：so good（太好了）、so warm（太溫馨了）、so delightful（太愉快了）。

以 so 引導子句的用法，請見規則 4。

> (✗) The one mile and two mile runs were won by Jones and Cummings respectively.
>
> (○) The one mile and two mile runs were won by Jones and by Cummings.

In some kinds of formal writing, as geometrical proofs, it may be necessary to use *respectively*, but it should not appear in writing on ordinary subjects.

 Should.

See under *Would*.

So.

Avoid, in writing, the use of *so* as an intensifier: "so good;" "so warm;" "so delightful."

On the use of *so* to introduce clauses, see Rule 4.

易誤用字詞 41 State（敘述）

不要直接用來代替 say（說）或 remark（評論）；state 的意思是「完整或清楚地表達」，例如：He refused to state his objections.（他拒絕說明反對的理由。）

易誤用字詞 42 System（體制；系統）

常是無須存在的冗詞。

（×）Dayton has adopted the commission system of government.

（○）Dayton has adopted government by commission.

達頓市透過委員會來治理。

（×）The dormitory system

（○）Dormitories（宿舍群）

State.

Not to be used as a mere substitute for *say*, *remark*. Restrict it to the sense of express fully or clearly, as, "He refused to state his objections."

 **System.**

Frequently used without need.

(✕) Dayton has adopted the commission system of government.

(◯) Dayton has adopted government by commission.

(✕) The dormitory system

(◯) Dormitories

易誤用字詞 43 Thanking you in advance
（先謝謝你／妳）

這句話讀起來會有「不必再聯絡了」的感覺。當你有求於人時，寫 Will you please（能否請您……）I shall be obliged（我將很感激）即可。待對方答應你的請求後，再回覆一封感謝函即可。

易誤用字詞 44 They（他們）

常見的錯誤是前面使用 each、each one、everybody、everyone 等單數形容詞或代名詞，後面卻使用複數代名詞 they 來指稱。另一個常犯錯誤是前面使用 anybody、anyone、somebody、someone，後面卻用 they 來代稱。

易誤用字詞 45 Very（非常）

慎用這個詞，試著用其他更有力的詞來加強語氣。❼

學習小提醒 7

直接使用表達更高程度的用語可以解決 very 的濫用情況，例如：very funny → hilarious（逗趣極了），更多範例請見「實戰練習手冊第 29 頁」。

Thanking You in Advance.

This sounds as if the writer meant, "It will not be worth my while to write to you again." In making your request, write, "Will you please," or "I shall be obliged," and if anything further seems necessary write a letter of acknowledgment later.

They.

A common inaccuracy is the use of the plural pronoun when the antecedent is a distributive expression such as *each, each one, everybody, everyone*, which, though implying more than one person, requires the pronoun to be in the singular. Similar to this, but with even less justification, is the use of the plural pronoun with the antecedent *anybody, any one, somebody, someone*.

45 Very.

Use this word sparingly. Where emphasis is necessary, use words strong in themselves.

易誤用字詞 46 **Viewpoint**（觀點）

建議寫成 point of view；別用來替代 view 或 opinion。

易誤用字詞 47 **While**（當……的時候）

不要隨意用 while 取代 and、but 或 although。許多人寫作時常用 while 來代替 and 或 but，可能是有意變換連接詞，或不確定要用 and 還是 but，在這種情況下使用分號為宜，例如：

（×）The office and salesrooms are on the ground floor, while the rest of the building is devoted to manufacturing.

（○）The office and salesrooms are on the ground floor; the rest of the building is devoted to manufacturing.

辦公室和賣場在一樓；其他樓層則專供生產製造之用。

在不會使語意模糊的情況下，while 可作 although 的意思用，例如：

 **Viewpoint.**

Write *point of view*, but do not misuse this, as many do, for *view* or *opinion*.

 While.

Avoid the indiscriminate use of this word for *and*, *but*, and *although*. Many writers use it frequently as a substitute for *and* or *but*, either from a mere desire to vary the connective, or from uncertainty which of the two connectives is the more appropriate. In this use it is best replaced by a semicolon.

(×) The office and salesrooms are on the ground floor, while the rest of the building is devoted to manufacturing.

(○) The office and salesrooms are on the ground floor; the rest of the building is devoted to manufacturing.

Its use as a virtual equivalent of *although* is allowable in sentences where this leads to no ambiguity or absurdity.

While I admire his energy, I wish it were employed in a better cause.

雖然我佩服他的幹勁，我希望他用在更有意義的事上。

也可寫成：

I admire his energy; at the same time I wish it were employed in a better cause.

我佩服他的幹勁；同時我希望他用在更有意義的事上。

再對照下面的句子：

（○）Although the temperature reaches 90 or 95 degrees in the daytime, the nights are often chilly.

雖然白天溫度可達華氏 90-95 度，晚上卻常涼颼颼的。

（×）While the temperature reaches 90 or 95 degrees in the daytime, the nights are often chilly.

當白天溫度達到華氏 90-95 度，晚上卻常涼颼颼的。

（×）The temperature reaches 90 or 95 degrees in the daytime; at the same time the nights are often chilly.

白天溫度可達華氏 90-95 度；同時，晚上常涼颼颼的。

用 while 改寫後，會發現與原意有出入，因此這樣的寫法是錯誤的。

我建議寫作時只採用 while 最原始的意義：「當……的時候」。

While I admire his energy, I wish it were employed in a better cause.

This is entirely correct, as shown by the paraphrase, I admire his energy; at the same time I wish it were employed in a better cause.

Compare:

(O) Although the temperature reaches 90 or 95 degrees in the daytime, the nights are often chilly.

(×) While the temperature reaches 90 or 95 degrees in the daytime, the nights are often chilly.

(×) The temperature reaches 90 or 95 degrees in the daytime; at the same time the nights are often chilly.

The paraphrase, shows why the use of *while* is incorrect.

In general, the writer will do well to use while only with strict literalness, in the sense of *during the time that*.

易誤用 字詞 48 Whom（關係代名詞 who 的受格）

同學寫作時常會在 he said 或類似句型前誤以 whom
代替 who。由於關係代名詞是動詞的主詞，因此應該
用 who。

（×）His brother, whom he said would send him
the money
（○）His brother, who he said would send him
the money
他說他哥哥會寄錢給他。

（×）The man whom he thought was his friend
（○）The man who he thought was his friend
（○）The man that whom he thought his friend
他以為是他朋友的那個人

易誤用 字詞 49 Worth while（值得的）

常被濫用為模糊表達贊同或不贊同的方式；這個用法
只能形容動作。

 **Whom.**

Often incorrectly used for *who* before *he said* or similar expressions, when it is really the subject of a following verb.

> (✕) His brother, whom he said would send him the money
> (◯) His brother, who he said would send him the money

> (✕) The man whom he thought was his friend
> (◯) The man who (that) he thought was his friend (whom he thought his friend)

49 Worth while.

Overworked as a term of vague approval and (with *not*) of disapproval. Strictly applicable only to actions: "Is it worth while to telegraph?"

（×）His books are not worth while.

（○）His books are not worth reading.

（○）His books are not worth one's while to read.

（○）His books do not repay reading.

（○）His books are worthless. 他的書不值得一讀。

易誤用字詞 50 Would（會，助動詞 will 的過去式）

第一人稱的條件句應使用 should，而非 would。

（×）I would not have succeeded without his help.

（○）I should not have succeeded without his help. 若沒有他的協助，我當時也不會成功。

在過去式動詞後面的間接引述中，shall 應改為 should，而非 would，如下頁例句：

(✕) His books are not worth while.

(◯) His books are not worth reading.

(◯) His books are not worth one's while to read.

(◯) His books do not repay reading.

(◯) His books are worthless.

50 Would.

A conditional statement in the first person requires *should*, not *would*.

(✕) I would not have succeeded without his help.

(◯) I should not have succeeded without his help.

The equivalent of *shall* in indirect quotation after a verb in the past tense is *should*, not *would*.

（×）He predicted that before long we would have a great surprise.

（○）He predicted that before long we should have a great surprise.

他預言我們不久後將有個大驚喜。

敘述習慣或重複的動作時，通常用過去式即可，不必多加 would，句子方能更簡潔有力。

（×）Once a year he would visit the old mansion.

（○）Once a year he visited the old mansion.

他每年都會造訪這間老宅一次。

(×) He predicted that before long we would have a great surprise.
(○) He predicted that before long we should have a great surprise.

To express habitual or repeated action, the past tense, without *would*, is usually sufficient, and from its brevity, more emphatic.

(×) Once a year he would visit the old mansion.
(○) Once a year he visited the old mansion.

以下這些易誤用字詞，
你都會分辨嗎？

- Due to 和 Owing to 的差別是什麼？

- 比較兩個本質相同事物的不同之處，要用 compare with 還是 compare to？

- who, which, when 這些連接詞前面，什麼時候 要加逗號？什麼時候不用？

- Less 和 Fewer 哪個是指程度，哪個是指數量？

- Data 和 Phenomena 的字尾可以加 s 嗎？

- Dependable 應該要用哪兩個同義詞取代？

- Divided into 和 Composed of 的差別是什麼？

- 由 Such as 和 For example 引導出的項目最後可 以使用 etc. 嗎？

- 為什麼在英文信件中道謝時，不應該使用 Thank you in advance？

65 個經常拼錯的單字

V

SPELLING

本章列出的單字大部分都不難，
有的甚至很常見，
卻連很多母語人士都會拼錯，
例如許多人往往會漏掉 embarrass 中的一個 r 或 s，
請讀者多加演練，避免犯錯。

英文的拼字法常隨時代改變，不服膺任何權威，而是在大眾的共識之下確立的。如今大部分的單字都有眾人一致認同的拼法。在下面列出的單字中，rime ／ rhyme（押韻；韻律）是唯一可通用的組合。即使在同一個時代，同一個單字仍可能有不同的拼法，但這些「特殊拼法」大都沒過多久便被淘汰。而隨著時代演變，新的單字、新的縮寫也不斷出現，有些贏得眾人的青睞，有些沒多久便銷聲匿跡。

讀者不認同是非主流拼法／用語消失的主要原因，因為這些拼法和用語會使讀者分心費勁、失去耐心。例如讀者讀到 though 時能一目瞭然，讀到其簡寫 tho 時卻還需要自行補字理解，結果寫作者「畫虎不成反類犬」了。

The spelling of English words is not fixed and invariable, nor does it depend on any other authority than general agreement. At the present day there is practically unanimous agreement as to the spelling of most words. In the list below, for example, *rime* for *rhyme* is the only allowable variation; all the other forms are co-extensive with the English language. At any given moment, however, a relatively small number of words may be spelled in more than one way. Gradually, as a rule, one of these forms comes to be generally preferred, and the less customary form comes to look obsolete and is discarded. From time to time new forms, mostly simplifications, are introduced by innovators, and either win their place or die of neglect.

The practical objection to unaccepted and over-simplified spellings is the disfavor with which they are received by the reader. They distract his attention and exhaust his patience. He reads the form *though* automatically, without thought of its needless complexity; he reads the abbreviation *tho* and mentally supplies the missing letters, at the cost of a fraction of his attention. The writer has defeated his own purpose.

常拼錯的單字列表：

accidentally	意外地
advice	建議 (n.)
affect	影響 (v.)
believe	相信
benefit	利益 (n.)；有利於 (v.)
challenge	挑戰 (n./v.)
coarse	粗糙的
course	課程；過程
criticize	批評
deceive	欺騙
definite	確定的
describe	描述
despise	輕視
develop	發展
disappoint	使……失望
dissipate	驅散；揮霍
duel	決鬥
ecstasy	狂喜
effect	效果 (n.)；招致；實現 (v.)
embarrass	使……尷尬
existence	存在
fascinate	使……著迷
fiery	火紅的；暴躁的
formerly	先前
humorous	幽默的
hypocrisy	偽善
immediately	立刻

accidentally

advice

affect

believe

benefit

challenge

coarse

course

criticize

deceive

definite

describe

despise

develop

disappoint

dissipate

duel

ecstasy

effect

embarrass

existence

fascinate

fiery

formerly

humorous

hypocrisy

immediately

impostor	騙子
incident	事件
incidentally	偶然；湊巧
latter	後者
led	導致（過去式）
lose	損失；輸掉
marriage	婚姻
mischief	淘氣；惡作劇
murmur	低語
necessary	必要的
occurred	發生（過去式）
opportunity	機會
parallel	平行的；並列的
Philip	飛利浦（人名）
playwright	劇作家
preceding	先前的
prejudice	偏見
principal	校長 (n.)；主要的 (adj.)
principle	原則；定律
privilege	特權
pursue	追求
repetition	重複
rhyme	押韻
rhythm	節奏；韻律
ridiculous	荒謬的
sacrilegious	褻瀆神明的
seize	抓住；理解

impostor

incident

incidentally

latter

led

lose

marriage

mischief

murmur

necessary

occurred

opportunity

parallel

Philip

playwright

preceding

prejudice

principal

principle

privilege

pursue

repetition

rhyme

rhythm

ridiculous

sacrilegious

seize

separate	使……分離 (v.)；分開的 (adj.)
shepherd	牧者
siege	圍困
similar	相似的
simile	明喻
too	也
tragedy	悲劇
tries	嘗試（第三人稱單數）
undoubtedly	無庸置疑地
until	直到
villain	惡霸

請注意，除 *v* 以外的單子音前方若有短母音重音，形成 -ed 或 -ing 字尾時必須重複子音，例如：planned、letting、beginning（coming 則是例外）。

separate
shepherd
siege
similar
simile
too
tragedy
tries
undoubtedly
until
villain

Note that a single consonant (other than *v*) preceded by a stressed short vowel is doubled before *-ed* and *-ing*: *planned, letting, beginning*. (*Coming* is an exception.)

記下自己經常拼錯的單字！

◎ 請在這頁寫下你曾經拼錯的單字或是片語，並
找出拼錯的原因，避免下次再犯錯！

24 個原版練習題及解答

EXERCISES ON CHAPTERS I AND II

以下是作者精心規劃的文法練習題，
特別針對第一、二章中的
１８大寫作規則來設計。
此外，編輯部更特別請
擁有多年寫作教學經驗的譯者陳湘陽老師，
提供專業解答給讀者參考。

PART 1 斷句練習：請為以下文章加入適當的標點符號

第 1 題

In 1788 the King's advisers warned him that the nation was facing bankruptcy therefore he summoned a body called the States-General believing that it would authorize him to levy new taxes. The people of France however were suffering from burdensome taxation oppressive social injustice and acute scarcity of food and their representatives refused to consider projects of taxation until social and economic reforms should be granted. The King who did not realize the gravity of the situation tried to overawe them collecting soldiers in and about Versailles where the sessions were being held. The people of Paris seeing the danger organized militia companies to defend their representatives. In order to supply themselves with arms they attacked the Invalides and the Bastille which contained the principal supplies of arms and munitions in Paris.

第 2 題

On his first continental tour begun in 1809 Byron visited Portugal Spain Albania Greece and Turkey. Of this tour he composed a poetical journal Childe Harold's Pilgrimage in which he ascribed his experiences and reflections not to himself but to a fictitious character Childe Harold described as a melancholy young nobleman prematurely familiar with evil sated with pleasures and embittered against humanity. The substantial merits of the work however lay not in this shadowy and somewhat theatrical figure but in Byron's spirited descriptions of wild or picturesque scenes and in his eloquent championing of Spain and Greece against their oppressors. On his return to England in 1811 he was persuaded rather against his own judgment into allowing the work to be published. Its success was almost unprecedented in his own words he awoke and found himself famous.

PART 2 練習解釋並修正錯誤的標點

第 3 題

This course is intended for Freshmen, who in the opinion of the Department are not qualified for military drill.

第 4 題

A restaurant, not a cafeteria where good meals are served at popular prices.—Advt.

第 5 題

The poets of The Nation, for all their intensity of patriotic feeling, followed the English rather than the Celtic tradition, their work has a political rather than a literary value and bears little upon the development of modern Irish verse.

第 6 題

We were in one of the strangest places imaginable. A long and narrow passage overhung on either side by a stupendous barrier of black and threatening rocks.

第 7 題

Only a few years ago after a snow storm in the passes not far north of Jerusalem no less than twenty-six Russian pilgrims perished amidst the snow. One cannot help thinking largely because they made little attempt to save themselves.

PART 3 指出下列句子的錯誤並修正 （可能有不只一種修改方式）

第 8 題

During childhood his mother had died.

第 9 題

Any language study is good mind training while acquiring vocabulary.

第 10 題

My farm consisted of about twenty acres of excellent land, having given a hundred pounds for my predecessor's lease.

第 11 題

Prepared to encounter a woman of disordered mind, the appearance presented by Mrs. Taylor at his entrance greatly astonished him.

第 12 題

Pale and swooning, with two broken legs, they carried him into the house.

第 13 題

Count Cassini, the Russian plenipotentiary, had several long and intimate conversations during the tedious weeks of the conference with his British colleague, Sir Arthur Nicholson.

第 14 題

But though they had been victorious in the land engagements, they were so little decisive as to lead to no important results.

第 15 題

Knowing nothing of the rules of the college or of its customs, it was with the greatest difficulty that the Dean could make me comprehend wherein my wrong-doing lay.

第 16 題

Fire, therefore, was the first object of my search. Happily, some embers were found upon the hearth, together with potato-stalks and dry chips. Of these, with much difficulty, I kindled a fire, by which some warmth was imparted to our shivering limbs.

第 17 題

In this connection a great deal of historic fact is introduced into the novel about the past history of the cathedral and of Spain.

第 18 題

Over the whole scene hung the haze of twilight that is so peaceful.

第 19 題

Compared with Italy, living is more expensive.

第 20 題

It is a fundamental principle of law to believe a man innocent until he is proved guilty, and once proved guilty, to remain so until proved to the contrary.

第 21 題

Not only had the writer entrée to the titled families of Italy in whose villas she was hospitably entertained, but by royalty also.

第 22 題

It is not a strange sight to catch a glimpse of deer along the shore.

第 23 題

Earnings from other sources are of such a favorable character as to enable a splendid showing to be made by the company.

第 24 題

But while earnings have mounted amazingly, the status of affairs is such as to make it impossible to predict the course events may take, with any degree of accuracy.

専業寫作 教師提供 **參考解答**

第 1 題

In 1788, the King's advisers warned him that the nation was facing bankruptcy; therefore, he summoned a body called the States-General, believing that it would authorize him to levy new taxes. The people of France, however, were suffering from burdensome taxation, oppressive social injustice, and acute scarcity of food, and their representatives refused to consider projects of taxation until social and economic reforms should be granted. The King who did not realize the gravity of the situation tried to overawe them, collecting soldiers in and about Versailles where the sessions were being held. The people of Paris, seeing the danger, organized militia companies to defend their representatives. In order to supply themselves with arms, they attacked the Invalides and the Bastille, which contained the principal supplies of arms and munitions in Paris.

第 2 題

On his first continental tour begun in 1809, Byron visited Portugal, Spain, Albania, Greece(,) and Turkey. Of this tour (,) he composed a poetical journal--Childe Harold's Pilgrimage, in which he ascribed his experiences and reflections not to himself, but to a fictitious character Childe Harold, described as a melancholy young nobleman prematurely familiar with evil, sated with pleasures, and embittered against humanity. The substantial merits of the work, however, lay not in this shadowy and somewhat theatrical figure, but in Byron's spirited descriptions of wild or picturesque scenes, and in his eloquent championing of Spain and Greece against their oppressors. On his return to England in 1811, he was persuaded rather against his own judgment into allowing the work to be published. Its success was almost unprecedented; in his own words, he awoke and found himself famous.

第 3 題

This course is intended for Freshmen <u>who</u> in the opinion of the Department are not qualified for military drill.

此句為限定用法，指涉那些「認為系所不夠格舉行軍演」的大學新鮮人，因此應刪去關係代名詞 who 前的逗號。

第 4 題

A restaurant, not a cafeteria,<u> where</u> good meals are served at popular prices.—Advt.

指涉的 Advt. 餐廳為專有名詞（僅有一個），因此應用補述用法，在 where 前方加上逗號。

第 5 題

The poets of The Nation, for all their intensity of patriotic feeling, followed the English rather than the Celtic tradition; their work has a political rather than a literary value and bears little upon the development of modern Irish verse.

The poets of The Nation, for all their intensity of patriotic feeling, followed the English rather than the Celtic tradition 已是一個完整句子，主詞為 The poets of The Nation，動詞為 followed。 their work has a political rather than a literary value and bears little upon the development of modern Irish verse 亦是一個完整句子，主詞為 their work，動詞為 has，連接兩個完整句子應用分號而非逗號。

第 6 題

We were in one of the strangest places imaginable: a long and narrow passage overhung on either side by a stupendous barrier of black and threatening rocks.

the strangest places imaginable 和 a long and narrow passage… threatening rocks 為同位語，因此須以冒號連接，冒號後首字須小寫。

第 7 題

Only a few years ago, after a snow storm in the passes not far north of Jerusalem, no less than twenty-six Russian pilgrims perished amidst the snow. One cannot help thinking largely, because they made little attempt to save themselves.

這兩個句子較長，須在語意完整處以逗號斷句，使語意更清晰便於讀者閱讀。

第 8 題

During childhood his mother died.
die 為「瞬間動作」，不可使用完成式，例如：

> （×）The first Chinese emperor, Qin Shi Huang, had died for 2200 years.
> （○）The first Chinese emperor, Qin Shi Huang, died 2200 years ago. 中國的第一位皇帝秦始皇死於 2200 年前，死不能「持續地死」。

第 9 題

Any language study is good mind training while <u>the learners are</u> acquiring vocabulary.

此句的 while 為「當……」之意，acquire vocabulary（習得字彙）前缺少主詞語意不清，容易誤會為 language study 在 acquire vocabulary，故應補上主詞 the learners。

第 10 題

My farm consisted of <u>some</u> twenty acres of excellent land, having given a hundred pounds for my predecessor's lease.

在名詞前的「大約」應該用 some/approximately 而非 about。

第 11 題

Prepared to encounter a woman of disordered mind, <u>he was astonished by the appearance presented by Mrs. Taylor at his entrance.</u>

分詞構句前後主詞須相同，後半句應使用 he 開頭改寫。

第 12 題

Pale and swooning, with two broken legs, <u>he was carried into the house.</u>

分詞構句前後主詞須相同，應以 he 開頭改寫後半句。

第 13 題

Count Cassini, the Russian plenipotentiary, <u>has had</u> several long and intimate conversations during the tedious weeks of the conference with his British colleague, Sir Arthur Nicholson.

此句句意強調 Count Cassini「曾經」和 Sir Arthur Nicholson 有過對話，因此應使用完成式。

第 14 題

<u>Though</u> they had been victorious in the land engagements, they were so little decisive as to lead to no important results.

開頭的 but 為冗詞，用 though 即可表示「即便」之意。

第 15 題

Because <u>I knew</u> nothing of the rules of the college or of its customs, it was with the greatest difficulty that the Dean could make me comprehend wherein my wrong-doing lay.

前半句的主詞是 I，後半句則是 the Dean，前後主詞不同應寫出，不可省略。

第 16 題

Fire, therefore, was the first object of my search. <u>Fortunately</u>, some embers were found upon the hearth, together with potato-stalks and dry chips. <u>Out of these</u>, with much difficulty, I kindled a fire, by which some warmth was imparted to our shivering limbs.

以 fortunately 表「所幸、幸運地」之意而非 happily。out of 可表示理由、來源或動機，例如 making love out of nothing at all（使愛無中生有）。

第 17 題

<u>With</u> this connection a great deal of <u>historical fact</u> is introduced into the novel about the past history of the cathedral and of Spain.

用 with 表「藉由」之意；歷史事實是 historical fact 而非 historic fact，historic 是「關鍵、重大」，而非「關於歷史」之意。

第 18 題

Over the whole scene hung the haze of twilight, which was so peaceful.

後半句的功能在於補充說明前半句的場景很 peaceful，因此應用補述用法。

第 19 題

Compared with Italy, living in (a country or region name) is more expensive.

應加入國家名，才能與義大利這個國家比較。

第 20 題

It is a fundamental principle of law to believe a man innocent until he is proven guilty, and once proven guilty, to remain so until proven to the contrary.

prove（證明）的過去分詞為 proven。

第 21 題

Not only did the writer have entrée to the titled families of Italy in whose villas she was hospitably entertained, but she also had entrée to royalty.

entrée 此指「入場權」，have（擁有）為動詞，因此倒裝時需使用助動詞 did，後半句讀起來語意不清，應以較清楚的方式改寫。

第 22 題

It is not strange to catch a glimpse of deer along the shore.

catch a glimpse 已有「看」的意思，因此 a strange sight 為冗詞，說 strange 即可。

第 23 題

Earnings from other sources are so favorable as to enable a splendid showing to be made by the company.

of such a favorable character 過於冗長，改為 so favorable 即可。

第 24 題

Though earnings have mounted amazingly, the status of affairs is such as to make it impossible to predict the events, with any degree of accuracy.

用 though 即可表示前後的讓步關係；the course events may take 為冗詞，說 predict the events 即夠清楚。

國家圖書館出版品預行編目 (CIP) 資料

英文寫作聖經：史上最長銷、美國學生人手一本、
常春藤英語學習經典 << 風格的要素 >> / 威廉·史
壯克 (William Strunk Jr.) 作；陳湘陽譯. -- 初版. --
新北市：野人文化出版：遠足文化發行, 2018.10
　面；　公分. -- (野人家；182)
中英對照
譯自：The elements of style
ISBN 978-986-384-316-0(平裝)

1. 英語 2. 修辭學 3. 寫作法

805.171　　　　　　　　　　　　　107015877

英文寫作聖經
《The Elements of Style》
線上讀者回函專用 QR CODE，你的
寶貴意見，將是我們進步的最大動力。

野人文化　　　野人文化
官方網頁　　　讀者回函

野人家 182

英文寫作聖經《The Elements of Style》

史上最長銷、美國學生人手一本、常春藤英語學習經典《風格的要素》
（中英對照，附原版練習題＆實戰練習手冊）
＊特別感謝譯者陳湘陽老師補充解說及範例

作　　者　　威廉·史壯克（William Strunk Jr.）
譯　　者　　陳湘陽

野人文化股份有限公司

社　　長　　張瑩瑩
總 編 輯　　蔡麗真
責任編輯　　陳瑾璇
專業校對　　林昌榮
行銷企劃　　林麗紅
封面設計　　莊謹銘
內頁排版　　洪素貞

出　　版　　野人文化股份有限公司
發　　行　　遠足文化事業股份有限公司(讀書共和國出版集團)
　　　　　　地址：231新北市新店區民權路108-2號9樓
　　　　　　電話：（02）2218-1417　傳真：（02）8667-1065
　　　　　　電子信箱：service@bookrep.com.tw
　　　　　　網址：www.bookrep.com.tw
　　　　　　郵撥帳號：19504465遠足文化事業股份有限公司
　　　　　　客服專線：0800-221-029
法律顧問　　華洋法律事務所　蘇文生律師
印　　製　　成陽印刷股份有限公司
初版首刷　　2018年10月
初版21刷　　2023年9月